ABSOLUTE POISON

ABSOLUTE POISON

Geraldine Evans

severn
House

This first world edition published in Great Britain 2002 by
SEVERN HOUSE PUBLISHERS LTD of
9–15 High Street, Sutton, Surrey SM1 1DF.
This first world edition published in the USA 2003 by
SEVERN HOUSE PUBLISHERS INC of
595 Madison Avenue, New York, N.Y. 10022.

British Library Cataloguing in Publication Data

Evans, Geraldine
    Absolute poison
    1. Rafferty, Detective Inspector (Fictitious character) - Fiction
    2. Llewellyn, Sergeant (Fictitious character) - Fiction
    3. Police - Great Britain - Fiction
    4. Detective and mystery stories
    I. Title
    823.9'14 [F]

    ISBN 0-7278-5914-5

Typeset by Palimpsest Book Production Ltd.,
Polmont, Stirlingshire, Scotland.
Printed and bound in Great Britain by
MPG Books Ltd., Bodmin, Cornwall.

*This book is dedicated to
my agent, Vanessa Holt, without whom . . .
Thanks, Vanessa. I owe you one.*

Prologue

'There'll be another one along in a minute' – wasn't that what they said? Inspector Joseph Rafferty gazed at the very dead old lady in the bed and mused that usually it was in respect of buses, not bodies.

But this week the bodies were bunched like the rush-hour double-deckers on Elmhurst's congested streets. The first suicide had been of a World War Two veteran whose suicide note had derided the notion that this was a land fit for heroes to live in. This old lady was the second suicide. And it was still only Wednesday morning. Rafferty, chock-full of Irish superstition, felt he could be forgiven for becoming equally chock-full of the conviction that they wouldn't get through the rest of the week without a third. As he remarked to Sergeant Llewellyn, in his experience, bad things always came in threes. It was a depressing thought.

Almost as depressing as the February weather, which, like the previous autumn, was as grey and dank as a dirty floorcloth. Even the jolly holly bush, with its urgent tap-tappings at the window, seemed to have had enough and to want to come inside for a warm. Hardly surprising the suicide rate was up.

Unlike the first suicide, on Monday, this one hadn't left a note. Not that there was anything unusual about that. Rafferty knew that only about a quarter of suicides left notes.

1

Pity stirred again as his gaze shifted from the aged cadaver in the bed to the stiffly posed sepia wedding photo on the mantelpiece. It showed a pretty young bride with glossy midnight-black hair, her arm possessively linked with that of the darkly handsome Brylcreemed groom.

Next to the wedding photo was another picture, presumably the bride and groom again, though now much older and unsmiling. Middle age hadn't changed the bride that much; in the later photo it was still possible to trace the girl she had been. Not so the groom. Middle age had transformed the slim young man into a bald gnome, red of cheek and jowly of jaw. There were pictures of a boy, too, presumably their son. His hair was fair and although he shared her dark eyes, his were solemn, not laughing like his mother's.

Rafferty sighed. The son would have to be found and notified. He dragged his gaze from the picture gallery and the smiling bride and back to the bed; to the old lady the bride had become.

The glossy black cap of hair was now thin, wispy, and grey. The slender hands, now calloused and work-roughened, were clasped neatly together outside the covers. Rafferty's gaze flickered over the scarred dresser with its empty pill bottles and the jug and glass both now scummy with clouded water, and he reflected on what it must be like to get so old and lonely that killing yourself became an attractive alternative to going on.

After routinely checking the body for any sign of life, he turned away and commented flatly to Llewellyn, 'There's nothing for us here.'

As soon as the words were out he was struck by how callous they sounded and felt ashamed. He realized he hadn't even asked her name before dismissing her and her passing. The trouble with such lonely deaths was that

2

they inclined him to melancholy for days. Experience had taught him that the only hope of escaping the glooms was by spending as little time as possible at the scene. Now he asked quietly, 'Who was she? Do you know?'

'The neighbours only knew her as Dodie.'

Rafferty nodded and beckoned Llewellyn on to the landing where the air was less redolent of death. 'The neighbours hadn't known her for long, then?'

'Some six months or so, I understand. Would you like me to check?'

Rafferty shook his head. 'No. It doesn't matter.' He added, more or less to himself, 'Six months and all they knew was that her name was Dodie.'

He wasn't altogether surprised. Half the street of terraced houses was boarded up to prevent squatters and vandals gaining access to empty properties. What had once been a friendly community was now an itinerant neighbourhood, the sort of place where your neighbours came and went without making a ripple in your life. Apparently, in this case, without even discovering more about you, your family and background than your first name. It was a sad indictment of modern life and did nothing to reduce Rafferty's gloomy feelings. 'She must have some papers,' he remarked and called down the stairs for Constable Smales to have a look for some. His voice, echoing loudly down the narrow stairs in this house of the dead, sounded oddly intrusive.

Llewellyn, unlike Rafferty, generally managed to retain a certain objectivity under such circumstances. 'Dr Arkwright should be able to tell us more. The neighbours were at least able to tell me he was the old lady's general practitioner as well as their own.' Rafferty nodded. Old Dr Arkwright had been practising in the town for around a third of a century, so would be able to put a surname to their suicide as well as provide details of any other family she might have had. 'Get on to him, Dafyd. Tell him what's happened and get him over here.'

'You're lucky you caught me,' Dr Obadiah Arkwright told them when he arrived twenty minutes later. 'I'm off to Scotland for a fishing holiday later today.'

He sounded tired, Rafferty noticed, and badly in need of his break. Obadiah Arkwright must be approaching seventy, but he was still an impressive-looking man; tall and saturnine of face, a tendency which age had made more marked, with an air of authority worn as easily as his ancient Sherlock Holmes style overcoat.

'Nice secluded spot,' Arkwright went on. 'As far from the joys of civilization as it's possible to get without either leaving the country or breaking the bank.' He paused. 'Upstairs, is she?'

Rafferty nodded and he and Llewellyn followed the doctor up the narrow stairs to the bedroom.

The doctor approached the bed and stared down at his late patient. After a quick examination he stood back and sighed. 'Poor woman. Of course, I know she's been depressed lately, but I never thought her the type to take this way out.' His quick gesture took in the empty bottle of sleeping tablets on the dresser.

'I thought we were all that,' Rafferty quietly remarked. 'All it needs is the right circumstances.'

'Not thinking of copying her example, I trust?' Arkwright asked, giving him an old-fashioned look.

But then he was an old-fashioned kind of doctor, Rafferty mused; the sort who had once existed in their hundreds. The sort whose patients clung to life as though not daring to leave it till the doctor had given his permission. The sort, too, who felt it their duty to check their

4

patients officially off their list and on to that of an even higher authority.

Rafferty forced a smile. 'Not me, Doc. Wouldn't dare. I might be a lapsed Catholic, but I'm still as leery of mortal sin as the biggest Bible-thumper.'

'What was her name, Doctor?' Llewellyn asked.

'Mrs Pearson. Mrs Dorothy Pearson.'

Glad to get a confirmed identification, Rafferty advised, 'I've had young Smales looking to see if he could find any personal papers in the house, but there are none. Looks like she had a grand clearing out before she took the overdose.'

'Doesn't surprise me,' said Arkwright. 'Mrs Pearson was a very private sort of person. Alone in the world, too. Probably didn't fancy strangers raking over her things. Her only son died earlier this year; not, in my opinion, that he was much of a loss.' The doctor raised expressive hands then let them drop. 'But there, I suppose for her, her son's death was the final straw. She's been alone for some time. She lost her husband years ago and then—'

He broke off as Sam Dally, part-time police surgeon cum pathologist, arrived with his usual noise and bustle. The grim little bedroom with its four- to five-day-old corpse was too small for all of them. Arkwright acknowledged Sam Dally, said his goodbyes and left. Rafferty and Llewellyn, after accompanying him down the stairs, waited in the living room for Sam to confirm their findings. He didn't take long. Nor, when he returned downstairs, did he pause to indulge in his usual ghoulish banter. Rafferty guessed that for Sam – who had lost his wife of thirty years to cancer only a month ago – the prospect of his own solitary old age was getting too close for comfort. He was certainly more irascible than usual, and briskly confirmed that Mrs Pearson had certainly been dead for the best part of a week. 'Early part of the weekend would be my estimate,' Dally added. 'Friday night probably, or Saturday morning.'

Rafferty had already guessed as much. His brief look under the bedclothes had revealed the tell-tale signs; the body swollen with gases, the skin blisters, the leaking fluids, the smell. He swallowed hard and waited for Sam to continue.

'Suicide, of course,' said Dally. 'Classic. Pills and whisky, but without the whisky. Don't suppose the poor bitch could afford that.' He gazed around the shabby living room with its clean but worn square of cheap carpet, the cramped, dark kitchen off, and added in lacklustre tones, 'I can't imagine there'll be any grasping relatives to fight over the family heirlooms.'

'No.' Rafferty reflected that even his ma, with her love of 'bargains', would find little here to interest her.

The funereal weather and the discovery of another lonely death were more than enough to get a man down. But thoughts of Ma and her 'bargains' reminded Rafferty that he had yet another reason to be gloomy; one that had, like the weather, been getting him down since Christmas. Unfortunately, unlike the weather, the cause of the other low depression was going to require some input from him. And as he walked back down Mrs Pearson's path, dodging puddles as he went, Rafferty reflected that a solution was as far away as ever.

Needless to say, his family were at the root of his problem. When weren't they? he murmured. Without his knowledge, his ma had persuaded Llewellyn to buy one of her dubious 'bargains' – a suit of quality as superior as its provenance and price were inferior. A suit which Rafferty had good reason to believe had formed part of an insurance fiddle by a tailor down on his luck.

Ignorant of both the suit's likely provenance and Ma Rafferty's back-of-the-lorry bargain-hunting propensities, Llewellyn had snapped up the suit. And, as Rafferty had afterwards learned, intended its first outing to be on the occasion of his wedding to Rafferty's cousin, Maureen.

Rafferty climbed in the car and wondered again how he was going to dissuade the Welshman from wearing the suit without revealing it was bent; a task made no easier given the first-class quality of its tailoring and the Beau Brummel tendencies of his sergeant.

With anyone else, of course, this wouldn't be a problem. With anyone else all he'd need to do would be to have a discreet word. Not with Llewellyn, though. Oh no, thought Rafferty. Nothing so simple. In fact, there was a distinct possibility that if he shared his suspicions the morally upright Welshman would shop Ma out of a sense of duty. Rafferty wished he didn't find it so easy to imagine Llewellyn explaining, quite kindly, that the law applied to everyone, even the mothers of detective inspectors.

Yet if he didn't tell Llewellyn, there was a good chance that someone at the wedding would admire the suit and ask Llewellyn where he had bought it. There were sure to be a fair number of their police colleagues at the reception and if one of them sniffed out the truth and it got back to Superintendent Bradley . . . But that possibility didn't bear thinking about.

It seemed a petty problem after the morning they'd had. But then, Rafferty had found that life was generally made up of an endless variety of such problems. Maybe it was the last in a long line of them that had prompted Dorothy Pearson to give up the struggle and bow out.

The unwitting catalyst of Rafferty's latest little poser climbed in the car beside him. After they had watched the mortuary van pull away, Llewellyn asked, 'Back to the station, sir?'

Rafferty nodded absently and sank back into his thoughts. For the umpteenth time he'd tried to make Ma see the error of her ways, but, as usual, his attempt had failed miserably.

'A suit's a suit,' she'd said. 'One's much the same as another. Though, seeing as you made such a fuss about its lack of labels, you'll be happy to know I sewed a Marks and Spencer tag in it.'

'St Michael?' Rafferty quoted the name of the store's old garment label. 'Patron Saint of Clothing? Oh well,' he had remarked tartly, 'that's my mind put at rest. No danger of anybody mistaking it for dodgy gear while St Michael's on guard duty.'

'It's only doing Dafyd a favour, I was,' Ma had told him indignantly. 'There's no need to get on your high horse. Sure and he'll have expense enough with this wedding without paying over the odds for a suit that Maureen's ma won't turn her nose up at. At least he'll have no worries on that score.'

'That'll be a comfort to him when he spends his honeymoon on remand in Costa del Pentonville.'

'Pentonville?' his ma had snorted. 'Don't be ridiculous. As if I'd sell Dafyd a suit likely to send him to prison.'

Rafferty had said no more, realizing it was a waste of breath. Ma was incorrigible. She would never give up her love of 'bargains', policeman son or no policeman son. His only consolation was that, as the wedding date had yet to be settled, he had time on his side. Anxious to confirm this happy state of affairs still existed, Rafferty adopted a casual tone as he asked Llewellyn, 'Named the day yet?'

Llewellyn didn't reply till he had negotiated the busy

junction by Elmhurst mainline train station. Then he said, 'It's not that simple. Maureen's a Catholic, like you. I'm a Methodist. And as my late father was a Methodist minister, my mother's sure to expect me to marry in that faith.'

Rafferty grinned. 'You mean Ma hasn't managed to convert you to Catholicism yet?'

Llewellyn shook his head.

'Must be losing her touch. Of course, these days her mind's taken up with other things than our love lives. She can hardly put it to anything else but my niece, Gemma, and the prospect of becoming a great-grandma in the summer. I'd take advantage of that, if I were you,' Rafferty teased, confident that the Welshamn's in-built dislike of haste would preclude him doing any such thing, 'and fix up a quick register office wedding before she's back to normal.'

Rafferty said no more. But now he relaxed back against his seat happy that religious differences and Llewellyn's natural caution would ensure the wedding was a long way off. It meant he had plenty of time to resolve the problem of the groom's dodgy suit.

One

C live Barstaple laced his fingers under his chin and stared out at his open-plan kingdom through the glass of his office window. The Big Brother overview had been installed on his instructions so the staff would know they were under his constant scrutiny. Most of them were now so cowed, so scared of losing their jobs, that one frowning glance through that shiny screen was enough to pale even the ruddy features of Hal Gallagher.

His kingdom. It might only be a temporary kingdom, but he still thought of it that way. His services as interim manager hired from his own consultancy firm which specialized in rationalization gave him that sense of potency, of power that he craved. He liked to watch all the little wage slaves, heads bowed, beavering away, knowing that his recommendation could secure their future – or ruin it. He'd put the fear of God into them all since his arrival three months ago. They were now all gratifyingly terrified that he'd think them slacking. Barstaple almost laughed out loud. The desire to laugh vanished abruptly, as, through his triumph, he heard the voice of his great-uncle in his head. It sounded sad and asked the question it always asked: 'Why do you want to hurt them?'

It was a question he had never answered. He didn't answer it this time. Always, he had veered away from delving too deeply into his own soul for fear of what he might find.

Instead, he forced his thoughts into more fruitful lines; such as the wisdom of his decision to turn his management skills to the growing rationalization market and specialize. His was a relatively easy job – lucrative, too; his brief to do the dirty jobs, like getting rid of staff, for which the in-house managers often had little stomach.

It was a simple enough exercise, the methods crude but effective. He was good at it, too, skilful at the chipping away of confidence, the repeated criticisms, the finding of weaknesses and using them for his own purposes. But then, he'd had a good teacher. The best.

In short, his brief was to intimidate, harangue, humiliate, till staff either provided him with a reason to sack them or left of their own accord. Of course, if the timescale had been briefer, he'd have had to use even cruder methods. But Plumley had given him six months, so he had time. And this way was so much more satisfying.

He caught the eye of Linda Luscombe, the nineteen-year-old blonde Head Office had sent over on work study from the local college, and gave her a proprietary smile as if he'd already possessed her. She flushed and dropped her eyes. Power was also an aphrodisiac, he'd discovered. It brought rewards in ways he had never fully appreciated. He was appreciating them now. Funny it had taken him so long. When he remembered what he'd had recourse to in the past . . . Again, he abruptly cut off the line of his thoughts.

She'd tried to pretend she didn't understand what he was after – and her with one illegitimate child already! Of course, when he'd made clear that the permanent post with the company when she'd finished college in the summer rested on his recommendation, she'd become much more anxious to please. After all, as he'd been at pains to make clear to all of them, jobs were hard to come by, for young women like Linda with unreliable child-minders as much as for the over-the-hill over-fifties. Most of them would find it out for themselves soon enough.

Of course they hated him. That didn't worry him. Let them hate, so long as they feared – wasn't it some Roman emperor who had coined the phrase? Whoever had coined it, Barstaple knew he'd been right.

He frowned and sent a minor tremor through the office before glancing at his watch. Nearly midday. Old Harris would be going to lunch any minute. Barstaple knew Harris had arranged to meet his wife in an attempt to patch up their marriage. Slowly, he unlaced his fingers; he intended to put a stop to that. It would never do to have the old dinosaur getting back to his wife just when he was on the point of cracking up and giving him an excuse to sack him.

Barstaple shouted Harris's name just as Harris headed for the door. 'Come in here a minute.'

Harris hesitated, then, his face a mask of apprehension, he turned and walked to the office door, with a gait that had become increasingly shuffling over the months. 'Yes, Mr Barstaple?'

'Come in here. I want a word.'

A quickly concealed dismay shadowed Harris's eyes, a touch of unexpected rebellion made him blurt out, 'I was just going to lunch, sir, and . . .'

'What's more important?' Barstaple asked silkily. 'Lunch or increasing the efficiency of the department? You seem to lack the team spirit, Harris. I've noticed that in you before. It's one of a number of things I've been meaning to discuss more fully with you and this seems an opportune moment.' He paused. 'Still, if your lunchbreak is more important to you . . .' He let the words hang on the air.

Harris blinked. For a moment Barstaple thought the old fool was going to burst into tears, as his Adam's apple bounced like a yo-yo against the corrugated skin of his throat. But then Harris got a grip on himself. His stiffened features revealed how tight a grip his emotions needed. The tightened lips muttered, 'No, sir. Of course not.'

Barstaple smiled. 'So glad you can spare the company a few minutes of your precious time. Come in and shut the door. We don't want to be disturbed, do we?'

Harris complied and then sank heavily into the hard chair, his air of defeat robbing Barstaple of much of his satisfaction. Until he noticed that Harris's lowered eyes held a simmering resentment rather than defeat. That was much better. The almost dumb insolence from the usually meek Harris send Barstaple's mind flying back years. Harris's face dissolved and instead, Barstaple found himself staring into the angry face of his father. He was again that small fearful boy, the boy his father had delighted in goading, in hurting. The face shimmered in front of suddenly tear-washed eyes. He blinked rapidly and when the tears had cleared, his father had gone and Harris's face was again before him, grey and anxious, and Barstaple felt a surge of relief swiftly followed by a desire to punish.

He decided to push Harris that little bit further. Who knew of what foolishness the man might be capable if he thought his last chance to patch up his marriage was being stolen from him?

*   *   *

13

It was thirty minutes later, just after half-past twelve, when Barstaple finally let Harris go. Long enough, he thought, for the estranged Mrs Harris to get good and mad at being stood up.

Harris, who had obviously come to the same conclusion, stood uncertainly in the middle of the open-plan office for fully ten seconds, before shuffling first to his desk and from there to the kitchen. He clutched a bag that probably contained the bland food, the milk and yoghurt that his ulcers demanded.

Barstaple remembered the large plate of peeled prawns he had waiting for him in the kitchen and his mouth watered in anticipation. They should have defrosted nicely by now. Shame he couldn't go to his usual restaurant for lunch, but he'd promised himself he'd lose a stone and there was no way he could do that if he carried on going to Luigi's every day. Besides, he thought as he glanced down at his lap-top, he wanted to get his report finished. It should do him a bit of good; maybe even earn him a fat bonus. If he continued as well as he'd started, he'd save Watts and Cutley a packet, especially as Plumley had had to tie his own hands to get Aimhurst's son to agree to the sale of the firm. And I'm the man with the golden key, he thought, the key to unlock those chains.

It was a few minutes later when he walked past the hunched figure of Harris. He was sitting at his desk sipping a glass of milk. Almost, Barstaple felt sorry for him, but he stopped that line of thought immediately. That way lay weakness. That way lay a return to the days of being a victim. He was resolved they would never come again.

He felt Harris's gaze follow him as he walked towards the kitchen; no doubt he was wondering what excuse he could give his wife, and Barstaple smiled to himself. It was true what they said, he reflected, there was more than one way to skin a cat. More than one way, too, to get rid of unwanted employees . . . Now – lunch. As he glanced again at Harris's defeated figure, he knew he'd earned it.

Two

After such a depressing day, Rafferty's one consolation that evening was that it was nearly over. In an attempt to cheer himself up, he planned an Indian takeaway, the latest video blockbuster from the States and the breaking open of a fresh bottle of Jameson's.

Fleetingly, he considered inviting one of the ladies of his acquaintance to share them with him and then abandoned the idea. He wasn't in the mood. Llewellyn's steady relationship with Maureen had brought home to him that his private life was as empty of fulfilment as that of the week's two suicides, and had been for months.

This realization destroyed his previous anticipation of quiet pleasures, so Rafferty wasn't altogether sorry when Sergeant Llewellyn's long face appeared round the door just as he was putting his coat on. Llewellyn told him that a man had been found dead in the offices of Aimhurst and Son, the light engineering firm on the roundabout.

'There,' Rafferty pronounced, with a kind of grim satisfaction. 'Didn't I tell you there'd be a third suicide?'

Llewellyn shut the door and came further into the office. 'We don't know yet that it is a suicide, sir. In fact . . .' he paused, then went on. 'PC Smales is there now and he says the dead man,' he glanced at a note, 'a certain Clive Barstaple, who was a hired consultant acting as an interim manager, was found slumped on his desk a

16

short time ago by one of the contract cleaners.' Llewellyn paused again and gave a delicate cough. 'PC Smales is of the opinion that Mr Barstaple had been poisoned.'

Rafferty stared at him. 'Since when did Smales become an expert witness? Or was the dead man found clutching a bottle marked poison?'

'No, sir.' Llewellyn's intelligent dark gaze was impenetrable. 'PC Smales has, he informed me, recently been doing some research on toxic substances. He hopes it will advance his career.'

Rafferty snorted. 'The only thing likely to do that is if he was planning to poison the entire nick.'

Llewellyn made no comment on Smales' ambitions and how they might best be achieved. 'He said that the dead man – the victim, as he insisted on calling him – exhibited the classic signs of rhododendron poisoning.'

Rafferty frowned. 'Are rhododendrons poisonous?'

'Every part of the plant is, I believe, highly toxic, sir.'

Rafferty's frown deepened. It was a new one on him. 'He didn't happen to mention what these symptoms are, by any chance? Only, unlike young Smales, I neglected my studies into the subject.'

'He says the symptoms include drooling, tearing of the eyes, nausea and vomiting, convulsions, diarrhoea, paralysis and coma. And – again according to Smales – the dead man had exhibited the more obvious symptoms as both his office and the lavatory show . . .' Llewellyn paused and gave a cough of even more delicacy, 'evidence of loss of bodily control.'

'Vomiting and diarrhoea must be symptomatic of any number of poisonous substances,' Rafferty pointed out. 'What makes Smales so sure he's right here?'

'I believe he mentioned the term "gut instinct", sir.'

'Gut instinct?' Rafferty's instinct was to snort again

17

and retort that the only gut instinct Smales was likely to experience was the usual male one when lusting after a pretty girl.

Just in time, he remembered that 'gut instinct' was his own invariable defence when he went bull-headed in pursuit of a favourite theory. Now, instead of making a sarcastic comment, he gazed thoughtfully at his sergeant and said, 'Good old gut instinct, hey? Never to be lightly ignored, even when it's Smales' gut that's getting all instinctive.' He got up. 'I suppose we'd better get over there and take a look. See if you can lay your hands on a book of toxicology, will you, Daff? There must be one around here somewhere. I'd like to check it out myself before I invite the world, his wife and Dr Sam Dally to find fault with our expert witness's deductions.'

'Smales said he had a copy in his locker.'

'And did he say where we might find the key?'

'He suggested we might try using a hairpin, sir.' Llewellyn gazed unblinkingly at him. 'He seemed to think you'd be familiar with the required technique.'

'Did he now?' Rafferty gave a sheepish grin. 'Maybe I ought to revise my opinion of young Smales. Come on, then.' He made for the door. 'I'll borrow the hairpin and you can bring the swag bag.' His grin widened as Llewellyn's features contracted. 'It's about time you learned the gentle art of breaking and entering.'

After checking quickly for any signs of life, Rafferty retreated to the doorway of Clive Barstaple's office, from where, with nostrils clenched, he gazed round the room. The smell, both in the small office and in the gent's toilet, was appalling. Obviously, in the later stages, Barstaple hadn't made it back to the lavatory; the dead man had not only soiled his trousers, he had vomited down his shirt as well as in the metal wastebin in the corner of the room. Apart from the swimming bile, the bin was half-full of shredded paper on top of which rested an empty yoghurt carton. The yoghurt was hazelnut flavour, Rafferty noted. It was the only one he liked.

The desk phone was off the hook, the receiver dangling down the side of the desk by its plastic wire, and Rafferty guessed the dead man had tried vainly to summon help. Obviously, he had left it too late and, presuming Smales' deductions to be correct, the convulsions and paralysis had overtaken him before he'd been able to do so. Rafferty could imagine that, in the earlier stages, the dead man had just assumed he had a particularly bad stomach upset and thought no more about it than to ensure he had a clear run to the lavatory. But then, as the symptoms had grown more violent he had probably been torn between lavatory and telephone.

Unfortunately for him, the need for dignity had triumphed over common sense until it was too late. Barstaple had died a horrible death, alone, frightened, covered in his own vomit and excrement. Poor bastard, thought Rafferty. Poor, poor bastard.

For the second time today, the odours of death overpowered him and he stumbled from the office, down the stairs and out into the fresh evening air. For once he didn't curse the weather. The cold raindrops refreshed him.

He was surprised to find that Llewellyn had followed him. Unlike his own, Llewellyn's stomach seemed able to take the most appalling sights and smells in its stride. To cover his attack of collywobbles, Rafferty now remarked, 'Seems like young Smales was right.'

Llewellyn nodded.

Though whether the culprit was rhododendrons or some other toxic substance, Rafferty wasn't prepared to hazard a guess. 'What a way to go. Somebody must have hated his guts to do that to him. Bloody awful death.'

Llewellyn nodded again. As if he sensed that Rafferty needed a few moments more to get himself together, he remarked quietly, 'The ancients were fond of poison, you know. Used it for murder, suicide, even judicial execution.'

Sensing an imminent lecture, Rafferty merely remarked, 'Is that so?'

'Oh yes. For instance, the Athenian philosopher, Socrates, was condemned to die on charges of atheism and corrupting youth. He was ordered to drink hemlock.'

Rafferty raised his eyebrows. 'And did he?'

Once more, Llewellyn nodded.

The information that one of Llewellyn's much-quoted and know-all heroes had got up other noses than his own and had met a sticky end for his pains restored Rafferty's stomach quicker than an Alka Seltzer. His manner more sprightly, he now remarked, 'And I thought your old Greeks and Romans were supposed to be such a civilized lot. God save us from civilized people, hey? Give me ignorant barbarians any day and a quick sword thrust in the vitals.'

Confident he now had his queasy stomach under control, Rafferty led the way back upstairs. This time, he was able to take in more than the immediately obvious. There was a large pinboard just outside the victim's office. It was covered with notices and he glanced at them; reminders to the staff of this or that new company policy; warnings of the penalties awaiting those who failed to grasp and implement the numerous changes swiftly; bans on smoking either inside or immediately outside the building, bans on eating outside the prescribed lunch periods, bans on making tea or coffee more frequently than lunchtime, once in the morning and once in the afternoon. The bans even extended to making more visits to the loos than the management deemed sufficient. The wording of all of them reminded Rafferty of Superintendent Bradley at his more pedantic. All were signed by the dead man. His earlier pity evaporating, Rafferty wondered sourly if Barstaple had issued a reprimand for his own recent overuse of the toilet facilities.

Barstaple's office was streamlined and functional. Its sole decoration, on the solid wall behind the desk, was several framed posters of some grey mechanical gadget called the Aimhurst Widget.

Rafferty, aware he'd have offended against nearly every one of Barstaple's dreary edicts, thought fondly of his own office, which in spite of Superintendent Bradley's frequent exhortations about tidiness, still remained as cosily ramshackle as ever.

Overcoming his distaste, Rafferty transferred his attention back to the dead man. The cadaver was half in, half out of his chair, which had tumbled to the floor with its load. Barstaple must have cracked his head as he fell, he thought, as he noted the skin on his forehead was broken. As it to confirm his conclusions, he now saw there was a smear of blood on the corner of the desk.

'Find out the name of the keyholder and get them over here, please, Dafyd,' he instructed. 'But before you do that, get on the blower and call Dally and the team out. When you've done that, have a word with the security guard on the desk. With a bit of luck he'll be an ex-copper and might have something useful to tell us. I'll speak to the woman who found the body. Where has Smales put her?'

'In the ground-floor staff room with the rest of the cleaners,' Llewellyn told him before heading off to make his phone calls.

21

Slowly, trying to compose his mind for the coming interviews, Rafferty followed him down the steep stairs to the ground floor and walked along to the staff room. Along with a collection of staff photographs, there was the same profusion of notices here as there had been in Barstaple's office. They even contained the same diktats.

WPC Green and PC Smales were there, along with the three members of the contract-cleaning firm. Smales was doing his best not to look smug and failing. His face, so boyishly smooth that Rafferty guessed he rarely needed to shave, was pink with excitement and Rafferty smothered a sigh.

The cleaners, two women and a man, stared anxiously at him. Incongruously, the male cleaner still sported a pair of bright yellow rubber gloves.

Rafferty nodded to Smales and after a quick, whispered, 'Well done. It looks as if you were right.' He added, in an attempt to curb some of Smales' more obvious adrenalin surge, 'I'll want you to take notes, Constable.' He spoke briefly to the contract-cleaning staff before asking, 'Which one of you found the body?'

'I did.' A plump middle-aged woman in a faded blue nylon overall answered.

'And you are?'

'Mrs Collins. Ada Collins.'

Rafferty was relieved to see that she seemed a sensible, level-headed kind of woman. Even after the shock of finding the body, she appeared remarkably composed and when Rafferty told her he'd like to speak to her first, she simply nodded and followed him down the corridor to the reception area.

The building was on two floors. It wasn't a large concern, and, as he now learned from a *sotto-voce* Smales, consisted of a reception area, conference room, four offices and a staff room on the ground floor, and a large open-plan office and male and female lavatories on the first floor. The open-plan office also incorporated a kitchen halfway down its length and the victim's own glassed-in office just inside the door.

As Llewellyn returned from his telephoning and took the security guard to an empty office, Rafferty led Mrs Collins to the seating area on the far side of reception. Smales sat importantly on the other side of her, notebook and pen much in evidence.

Although composed, Ada Collins had had an unpleasant experience and Rafferty spent the first few minutes gently drawing her out about herself before he led her on to the discovery of Clive Barstaple's grisly death. 'What time did you find the body?'

'It was about six thirty.' She blew her nose firmly with a large, practical, man's handkerchief before stuffing it back in her overall pocket. 'In the normal way of things I wouldn't have been the one to find him at all. I don't usually do this floor,' she explained. 'Only Dot – Mrs Flowers, the regular cleaner – had some family trouble last week. Her lad.' She shook her head sympathetically. 'From something she let slip one time, he's obviously a bit of a handful. Drugs,' she added darkly. 'Poor Dot had to pay his fine last time. He's in hospital up in Birmingham. Overdose, I shouldn't wonder. Anyway, Dot said she was going up there and wouldn't be in to work on Monday.'

'When did she ring you?'

'Friday night.' Mrs Collins paused and clenched her work-thickened fingers together in her lap before adding, 'You never know what trouble's waiting for you, do you? Thank God my lads are no bother.'

'Did she say what hospital her son was in?'

Mrs Collins shook her head. 'She didn't say a lot at

23

all. She's never been a chatty woman at the best of times and with getting such news it was hardly that, was it? And her on her own, too. I dare say the boy's missed a firm hand.'

Rafferty nodded.

'Anyway, as I said, she rang me and told me she didn't expect to be in all this week, so I rang the boss, Mr Arnold, Ross Arnold – he owns Allways Cleaning Services – and he sent Mrs Chakraburty to cover. Only she's not so good on her legs – she told me she had rickets when she was young, and can't manage stairs very well – usually she does one of the local supermarkets – so I said I'd do the first floor.'

'I see.' Rafferty paused. 'I gather from my constable here that Mr Barstaple – the dead man,' he added as he saw her blank expression, 'was collapsed over his desk when you found him?'

'That's right. I thought he was just feeling poorly and taking a nap as he was slumped on the desk with his head on his arms. I didn't notice the mess in the bin or on his clothes at first – my eyesight's poor, you see and my sense of smell was never what you could call good. I didn't want to startle him when I turned on the hoover, so I gave him a shake to wake him. But as it turned out it was me who had the start. As I told your young officer –' she nodded at Smales who blushed and buried his head back to his notebook – 'I just shook the poor man by the shoulder, and the next thing I knew, he'd tumbled to the floor, chair and all.'

She paused, took a deep breath and carried on. 'I hadn't been able to see his face before. It gave me quite a turn, I can tell you.' She pulled her handkerchief from her pocket again and, after blowing her nose, gripped the cotton square tightly. 'Poor man, and him so young. Still,'

24

she added brightly, 'gastric can be a terrible thing and there's been a lot of it around lately. I suppose it strained his heart?'

Rafferty made no comment on this. 'I gather you didn't know him personally?'

Ada Collins shook her head. 'No. The staff were usually gone by the time we got here. Sometimes, one or two would be working late, but I never saw this man before. Barstaple you said his name was?'

Rafferty nodded.

Her lips pursed at this and her gaze narrowed thoughtfully. 'I remember now; he was the one nobody liked. I'd once or twice overheard some of the staff talking about him,' she explained. '"Barstaple the Bastard", they called him.'

Rafferty glanced at Smales, who had been frantically scribbling to keep up. But as Mrs Collins said this he looked up with shining eyes. His expression said it all. What did I tell you, sir? it said. Someone's murdered him.

Rafferty's gaze narrowed warningly and Smales dropped his own back to his notebook.

'What did you do then?'

'I let out such a yell that the others came running – even Mrs Chakraburty.' Ada Collins gave a shaky laugh. 'I found a mouse earlier this year – I can't bear the creatures,' she explained, 'and I suppose they thought I'd found another one. Anyway, up they came, Mrs Chakraburty and Eric and Albert, the security guard. Albert shooed us all out and made us wait down here while he rang 999. I did try to tell him we ought to try to res . . . resusc – bring him back to life – but Albert just kept saying not to bother trying as he was way past our help.'

'So you were the only one to go up to the first floor before the discovery of the body?'

Ada Collins stared at him, the unexpectedly clear periwinkle-blue eyes looking out of place in the worn, middle-aged face. 'What difference does that make?' she finally asked. 'He died of a heart attack – didn't he?'

'We'll have to wait for the pathologist to determine cause of death, Mrs Collins. But, in the meantime, we have to check certain facts, like who was up on that first floor between the time the staff left – at five thirty?' She nodded. 'When he was presumably still alive – and the time you found him just after six thirty. Should this turn out to be an unnatural death we need to eliminate as many people as possible.'

Ada Collins took a few seconds to digest this. Then she paled and stammered, 'You mean – you mean you think somebody murdered him?'

Rafferty made no answer to this. She didn't seem to expect one. 'Did anyone else but you go up to that floor?' he repeated.

'Only Eric. Eric Penn, one of the other cleaners. You met him downstairs. Anyway, he came up earlier to make the tea. We always start with a cup and Eric always makes it. He's a bit simple, but there's no harm in him and he's a hard worker which is why Mr Arnold agreed to keep him on when the previous owner sold the cleaning business.'

'And Mr Penn didn't notice anything amiss?'

She shrugged. 'If he did, he said nothing to me. If he noticed him at all he probably thought, like me, that he was asleep. Of course, the door was shut, so any smell . . .' She came to an embarrassed halt.

Rafferty was surprised to learn that the door to Barstaple's office had been closed. He'd assumed that, feeling so ill, the dead man would have wanted an unrestricted path to the toilet. If Barstaple had been poisoned, and if Smales' gut instinct should prove to be correct and it was the toxic substance in the rhododendron plant that had done the job, it must have been administered long before the cleaners arrived. According to Smales' book of toxicology, the toxic substance in the plant took around six hours to work.

'By the way,' Rafferty asked, 'can you let me have Mrs Flowers' address? Just for the record.'

She shook her head. 'I don't know it, though I've an idea she lives near the station, but exactly where . . .' She shrugged. 'She won't be there, anyway. She'll still be up in Birmingham with her son.'

'Never mind. I imagine your employer will know it.' Rafferty drew the interview to a close. He didn't want Ada Collins chatting to her colleagues, so as she left and Smales went to follow her, Rafferty called him back and told him softly, 'Put her into an empty office, put Hanks on the door and send Mrs Chakraburty along in five minutes. Oh, and send Sergeant Llewellyn in your place. He should be finished with the security guard by now.'

'But, sir—' Smales started to protest at what he evidently regarded as the stealing of his thunder.

'Not now, Smales. We've too much to do.'

Smales went off trailing a long sigh. Two minutes later Llewellyn appeared.

'Get anything useful from the security guard?' Rafferty asked.

Llewellyn shook his head. 'It was just as Smales said. The supervisor of the contract cleaners found the body, screamed and brought everyone else running. The security guard isn't an ex-policeman, but he acted sensibly and secured the scene of death and gathered everybody downstairs in the staff room while he phoned us.'

Rafferty nodded.

'The keyholder's been informed. He's the deputy manager, a Mr Gallagher. Said he'd be about half an hour and Dr Dally and the scenes of crime team are on their way.'

Rafferty nodded again and told Llewellyn about Barstaple's nickname. But before Llewellyn could comment, there was a knock on the door and Smales put his head round and announced Mrs Chakraburty.

Mrs Chakraburty was a small and slight Asian woman. Painfully shy, with poor English, she seemed scared out of her wits and Rafferty had to coax the answers from her. Even then, her accent was so strong he had trouble understanding her. He found he had to listen intently to understand her at all.

She merely confirmed what Mrs Collins and the security guard had told them. It was clear they were going to get no hints of staff gossip from Mrs Chakraburty. After checking they had her address, he told Llewellyn to escort her back downstairs and to bring Eric Penn up.

Eric Penn was quite young, about twenty-five, and built like an ox. He seemed very restless and shuffled constantly on his chair as if he couldn't get comfortable. His eyes flickered continually between Rafferty and Llewellyn.

Rafferty couldn't decide whether Eric was excited or terrified, though the way he hugged his arms across his body would seem to indicate the latter. As he said Eric's name, the man's eyes settled on Rafferty with an unblinking stare that was quite unnerving. Rafferty hurried on with his questions.

Unfortunately, Eric Penn was not the sort of person it was possible to hurry. He needed as much encouragement as Mrs Chakraburty and even then his answers were so garbled and uncertain that Llewellyn said afterwards that he had the feeling Eric was holding something back.

After he had confirmed what the others had said, Rafferty remarked encouragingly, 'I understand that Mr Barstaple, the dead man, had a nickname?'

Eric grinned and suddenly became much more voluble. 'Bast'le the Bastard,' he told them loudly. 'Do you know what bastard means?' he asked as though he was about to confide a secret. 'I do. Shall I tell yers?'

Rafferty stared at him, appalled and saddened by his damaged humanity and he said gently, 'Thank you, Eric, but we know what it means.'

The faint light that had enlivened Eric's dull features went out again. 'Just thought I'd tell yer. Iffen you didn't know.' He paused, then burst out, 'He was an' all. A bastard. Called me an effin' moron once.' His face puckered. 'That's not nice, is it? Not a nice thing to call me.'

'No, Eric, it's not. You didn't like him, then?'

Eric shook his head vehemently.

'Did you often see him working here in the evenings?' Ada Collins had told him she didn't know the dead man, had never met him. Yet it was obvious from what Eric had told him that Barstaple must occasionally have encountered the cleaners.

Eric shook his head, but didn't add anything more. Rafferty had to press him before he discovered that, after that one occasion when Eric had been cleaning the stairs and had earned the cruel moron rebuke for not getting out of Barstaple's path quickly enough, Eric had generally taken trouble to keep out of his way.

Rafferty tried once more to gain Eric's confidence. With a smile, he remarked, 'Mrs Collins says you're a hard worker.'

This brought a broad grin to Eric's face. Sadly, the grin made him look even more simple. 'I am. I'm a good boy. Mum told me I'd have to work hard and I do. I do work hard. Mrs Flowers told me I clean better than anyone else,' he told Rafferty proudly. 'And faster.'

Probably for poverty wages, Rafferty guessed. Still, his needs were probably few – not that that was an excuse for exploitation. Rafferty asked if he had seen Clive Barstaple this evening and Eric nodded.

'Asked him iffen he wanted a cup of tea. But he never answered, though I asked him three times. That was rude, wasn't it?'

Rafferty nodded. Barstaple had undoubtedly been dead by then, but he didn't mention this probability to Eric. 'I'm surprised you offered to make him tea when he'd been so unkind to you. Why did you do that, Eric?'

Eric looked confused at this and eventually he mumbled, 'Mum learned me my manners.'

Llewellyn popped a question into the pause. 'Didn't you notice the smell, Eric? The office bin was full of vomit and he'd—'

'Course I did. It ponged.' Eric pulled a disgusted face. 'Dirty. Should have used lavvy. I shut the door to keep the pong in.'

'So it was open when you went up to make the tea shortly after you arrived this evening?' Llewellyn asked.

Eric nodded.

That was one thing cleared up, anyway, thought Rafferty.

WPC Liz Green knocked and advised them that Dally and the SOCO team had arrived. Rafferty told Eric to go with Liz and wait with the others. He seemed reluctant to go. Barstaple's death had apparently excited him and it was clear that he shared Smales' juvenile desire to be where the action was. Rafferty had to be quite firm with him to get him to do what he'd been told.

'Young Smales seems full of himself,' Sam Dally complained as he divested himself of his overcoat, hat and woolly tartan scarf in the reception area. 'Told me yon cadaver was likely poisoned by the toxins in the rhododendron plant. Is he after my job, do you reckon?'

Rafferty smiled. 'I reckon you're safe enough, Sam. It's only toxicology he's been studying, not pathology.'

'Toxicology, is it?' Sam smoothed the hair around his bald spot and remarked silkily, 'Then you'll be glad to know I did my bit to extend his education in that direction. Do you know, Rafferty, he was nae aware that there are poisons so subtle they leave no trace in the human body?'

'Is that so?'

'Och, yes. Your clever sergeant reads the classics so probably knows all about them. There's one – the name escapes me for the minute – where the only thing the body tells you when you cut it open is that the victim died of asphyxia. I was only saying to young Smales that it's a curious thing, but it's my experience that these particular poisons work best on wee young smart-arses. Strange that.'

Sam seemed tickled that he'd been able to indulge his heavy-handed and barbed humour at Smales' expense. He beamed, struggled into his protective gear and picked up his bag. 'So where's the body? I gather you do still want my opinion now that I'm here? I wouldn't like to feel I'd entirely wasted my evening, you having such an undoubted expert on hand and all.'

Three

B y the time Sam had finished his examination of the body he was forced to concede that Smales' conclusions might – just possibly – be right.

'That is, as far as the victim being poisoned is concerned,' he added. 'As to the means, unlike Smales, I prefer to make my conclusions from facts, not guesswork. I don't know what I might find when I get him on the table.'

Aware that Sam's professional ego had been bruised and that he was consequently reluctant to concede that the rest of Smales' conclusions might also be correct, Rafferty was forced to press him. 'But you do think it possible he died of carbohydrate andromedotoxin poisoning?'

'Haven't I just said so?' Dally scowled and his rimless spectacles glinted as he bit out the words. 'Could also be several other things, like an amphetamine overdose, or water hemlock or—'

'Hemlock?' Rafferty repeated, as he remembered Llewellyn's earlier titbit.

'Amongst other possibilities,' said Sam testily. 'There are quite a number of things that cause vomiting and diarrhoea, which is why I, unlike your resident expert, prefer to wait before jumping to conclusions. So, if you want any more information now,' Sam paused and pulled off his gloves with a resounding snap, 'I suggest you consult Constable Timothy Smales. He seems to be the man with all the answers round here.'

'Not quite all,' Rafferty commented drily. 'He doesn't know what subtle poison you're likely to use on him for his presumption.'

'That's true.' Sam's glasses glinted again. 'I must remind him of that on my way out.' He paused, rocked back on his heels and gazed at Rafferty with a narrowed gaze. 'Just supposing Smales is right – just supposing, mind,' he repeated. 'Did yon young smart-arse happen to mention how long, from ingestion to reaction time, carbohydrate andromedotoxin takes to do its stuff?'

'No,' Rafferty lied. 'He couldn't remember.' He wanted cooperation not aggravation and discretion was more likely to get it for him. It was always a hard enough balancing act to get Sam to commit himself to much before the post-mortem without making life difficult for himself. Rafferty regarded it as a challenge to his powers of persuasion to get him to say anything definite; it was as much a matter of professional pride with him as medical matters were for Sam. Fortunately, Sam's next words told him he'd struck just the right note.

'Och. These amateurs.' Sam jammed his hat on his head with a triumphant flourish. 'The poison is one of the most toxic you can find. A very small amount of it kills – just seven drops will do it. From ingestion to reaction time is around six hours.'

'Six hours?' Rafferty frowned as, for Sam's benefit, he did some pretend arithmetic. 'So he'd have taken it around lunchtime?'

'So my calculations would indicate. Of course, I can't speak for yours. Maths never was your strong suit, was it, Rafferty?'

Rafferty gave a strained smile. Even though it seemed

33

he'd been given a reprieve on the dodgy suit question, it was still a sore point and Sam's unfortunate choice of the s-word rubbed the sore spot all over again. Luckily, Sam didn't appear to notice anything, though Llewellyn gave him an odd look.

'Anyway,' Sam went on, repeating, practically word for word, Smales' earlier recitation of the symptoms, 'amongst other things, the victim suffers a slow heart-beat, hypertension, nausea and vomiting, diarrhoea, convulsions and paralysis. They finally slip into a coma. If carbohydrate andromedotoxin is what killed him, I imagine he put the earlier symptoms down to some kind of bug and wouldn't be unduly alarmed.'

Rafferty nodded. That was something else he'd already deduced.

Sam smiled with a return of his usual black humour and added, 'He'd be more concerned with getting to the lavatory, and then, by the time the convulsions and paralysis took hold, and the realization came to him that he was seriously ill, he would be unable to get help.' He shook his head. 'A nasty death. A very nasty death.'

'Around lunchtime,' Rafferty repeated thoughtfully.

As though suspecting Rafferty's repetition of the phrase questioned his judgement, Sam remarked tartly, 'Such is my humble prognosis, though if you'd like a second opinion . . .' He let the words hang in the air as he tightened his scarf with force enough to strangle a lesser man.

Although he was inclined to tease the irascible Scot by saying he'd consult Smales, Rafferty judged it prudent to forgo the pleasure and he shook his head. Sam's recent bereavement had increased his irritability and nowadays the only teasing he could stomach was his own.

'No?' Sam gave him a tiny smile which told Rafferty

the doctor knew perfectly well the extent of his temptation. 'Very well. In that case, I'll make an effort to carry out the post-mortem this evening.' He paused and produced another smile, one that didn't bode well for somebody. 'And seeing as young Smales has such a particular interest in the case it would be a kindness to let him attend.'

Like Rafferty, Smales did his best to avoid post-mortems. But, unlike Rafferty, Smales, with the carelessness of youth, had neglected to keep this repugnance to himself.

It was clear Sam was going to make sure that in future Smales thought twice about trying to steal his professional thunder. Rafferty, who had tried and failed on various occasions to get Smales to control his schoolboy enthusiasm for corpses – whole ones, anyway – wasn't averse to trying a harsher method.

'You know me, Sam,' he remarked airily. 'Like you, I'm all for encouraging the young. Of course he can go. Just give me time to wheel in a replacement.'

Sam, not being a believer in compromise, went for the full complement of victims. 'You'll be there, of course?'

Rafferty made his excuses. 'Afraid I've got too much to do at this end.' Besides, he was damned if the old bugger was going to get two sacrificial victims for his officially sanctioned sadism. 'Seems our late cadaver is not only likely to be seriously unlamented, but would have brought up the rear in a popularity contest that included the entire ranks of both Labour and Tory parties. Anyway,' he added waspishly, as Sam's knowing grin made him forget his earlier wise resolution, 'you'll hardly need me. Not with young Dr Smales there to hand you your knives.'

Thankfully, just then, Llewellyn interrupted to let

35

Rafferty know that the keyholder had arrived and he was able to make his escape before Sam was tempted to stick a knife into *him*.

'So what killed him?' In the way of Americans, Hal Gallagher, the keyholder and deputy manager, was upfront with both curiosity and questions.

Rafferty was surprised to find an American at such a small firm; he had always considered them a go-getting people and he thought it unlikely go-getting tendencies would find much scope at Aimhurst and Son.

Although now obviously pushing sixty, with little worry lines radiating out from his eyes, Hal Gallagher still had a fresh-faced ruddiness that was more usually seen in a younger man. He had a rangy figure that would look more at home riding a horse than an office chair. 'Was that guy I saw going out the sawbones?'

Rafferty nodded. He wondered how long the American had lived in England; he had certainly lost little of his accent, which sounded as rough as the Brooklynese Rafferty was familiar with from the American films he had devoured in their hundreds in his youth.

He drew Gallagher along the corridor to the empty office. Llewellyn followed. 'You must prepare yourself for a shock,' Rafferty said. 'I'm afraid Clive Barstaple was almost certainly poisoned. Of course, we'll know for sure after the post-mortem.'

Gallagher whistled softly. 'You mean somebody waste-killed him, I take it?'

Rafferty was amused at Gallagher's gangsterese. It sounded like a throwback to an earlier era and he wondered if the American had consciously adopted more vigorous expressions as a way of retaining his identity so far from home. 'Let's put it this way – he's dead, and if our supposition as to the cause is correct, no one in their right mind would choose this particular poison as a means of suicide. Nor does it seem likely that Mr Barstaple took it by accident.' Rafferty paused. 'You don't seem very surprised, Mr Gallagher.'

Gallagher shrugged. 'I guess I'm not. Clive wasn't a real nice guy.'

Rafferty nodded. 'Tell me, sir, have you any idea what else – apart from the nut yoghurt that was discarded in his wastebin – Mr Barstaple might have eaten today?'

Gallagher frowned. 'There was a large dish of prawns defrosting in the kitchen this morning. I guess they were Clive's. He generally went out for lunch, but he's been on a diet for the past few weeks and tended to stick with the kind of stuff that didn't need cooking, like supermarket prawns, smoked salmon and so on. Nothing but the best for Clive.'

Rafferty nodded again. Seemed Barstaple's diet was a happy coincidence for somebody. He'd already checked the kitchen. There were no dirty dishes in the sink. He mentioned as much to Gallagher. 'Would Mr Barstaple have washed the plate and cutlery himself?'

Gallagher laughed. 'Hell, no. Clive do dishes? No way. At most, he'd have stacked them in the sink for the cleaners.'

Maybe Eric Penn had cleared them away while he was waiting for the kettle to boil, thought Rafferty. He asked Llewellyn to check it out.

There was a short silence which Gallagher broke. 'Perhaps I ought to warn you to expect a visit from Watts and Cutley's big cheese, Alistair Plumley. I can't say when exactly, but I left messages all over for him when your sergeant rang me with the news of Barstaple's death.'

Rafferty frowned. 'Watts and Cutley?' The firm was well-known and had various branches up and down the country. Rafferty didn't understand what they could have to do with this case and said as much.

'We were taken over by them four months ago,' Gallagher explained.

'I see.' Even if Watts and Cutley had taken Aimhurst and Son over, Rafferty thought it odd that Gallagher should have so quickly informed the boss of the parent company of Barstaple's death, especially as, at the time of the phone call, it hadn't been confirmed that the death was suspicious. The close-mouthed Llewellyn would certainly not have let such a detail slip. 'Is it usual to immediately notify a man of Mr Plumley's importance when an employee dies on the premises?'

Gallagher laughed again. Rafferty wondered if it was his imagination that the American's manner seemed more uptight than before.

'No, of course not. But Clive Barstaple was his man; reported directly to him. My job would be on the line if I didn't tell him asap. Alistair Plumley doesn't like people dying on the premises, Inspector, from whatever cause. Apart from being bad for the company image, it shows a sad lack of team spirit – Watts and Cutley are hot on team spirit. Plumley likes his employees to die in their own time and on their own premises, not those of the company.'

Rafferty couldn't help wondering – if dying a natural death on Watts and Cutley's premises was regarded as showing a sad lack of team spirit – in what light an employee who had the temerity to get himself murdered there would be regarded. But rather than comment on this, Rafferty restricted himself to expressing surprise that such a large and diverse concern as Watts and Cutley should be interested in a small firm like Aimhurst and Son.

Gallagher enlightened him. 'The best things come in

small packages, Inspector, isn't that what they say? In this case, Watts and Cutley wanted to get their hands on a nifty little mechanical gadget we hold the patent on – the Aimhurst Widget, to give it its non-technical name. This gadget is used in any number of household appliances and our workshop in Lincoln churns them out in their hundreds of thousands. It's a very profitable line. So when Robert Aimhurst, the founder of the firm, died last year, they saw their chance, moved in and made his son a very attractive offer which, unfortunately for us, he chose to take. Which is how Clive Barstaple came on the scene as interim manager. His unofficial brief was rationalization.'

Rafferty nodded. Rationalization was, he knew, just one of a whole dictionary of euphemisms used by bosses to avoid the use of more emotive expressions. Nowadays, instead of being fired you were *iced* or forced into an *involuntary career event*. You weren't made redundant, you were *downsized* or *de-hired*.

Rafferty had no time for the minds and attitudes that had created such expressions. As if the dole queue by any other name wouldn't still smell of poverty, deprivation and despair.

'*Unofficial* brief, you said?'

Gallagher nodded. 'I guess Gareth – Robert Aimhurst's son – had just enough regard for the old guy to insert a clause into the deal with Watts and Cutley guaranteeing the continued employment of the current workers, unless they gave due cause for dismissal – that's where Clive Barstaple and the unofficial rationalization came in.'

Llewellyn interrupted. 'Excuse me, sir, but how did you know about this clause? Was it generally known?'

Gallagher nodded. 'I made it my business to spread the knowledge around once I knew. When the takeover was announced, I took young Gareth out and got him drunk so I could find out the ins and outs of the deal. It didn't take more than a couple of large ones. He blabbed it all out, seemed to think me and the rest of the staff should be grateful he'd spared us a thought. As if we didn't know the bottom line of the deal as well as he did. Large concerns like Watts and Cutley always find a way to ease out staff they don't want. And they have; three have left since Christmas, two of them on the verge of nervous breakdowns. Another one is managing to cling on, though taking such a combination of painkillers, antidepressants and sleeping pills he's likely to rationalize himself out of the world, not just the job. Not bad going in a few short months.'

Llewellyn interrupted again. 'Did nobody make representations to senior management about Mr Barstaple's methods? I would have thought you could have used this clause you mentioned as a bargaining counter.'

Gallagher looked steadily at him. 'What would be the point? They were the ones who wrote Clive's brief. Watts and Cutley wanted rid of the bulk of the staff without contravening Gareth Aimhurst's clause and laying themselves open to possible financial penalties. It's my guess they gave Barstaple six months to do it.'

'Did none of the staff who resigned consider pursuing the matter through an industrial tribunal? From what you say, the way they were forced out amounts to constructive dismissal.'

Currently hypersensitive on the subject of dismissal, whether constructive or otherwise, Rafferty gave a cynical laugh. 'And who would be likely to employ them in the future if they had something like that on their work record?' he demanded. Thoughts of Superintendent Bradley and the 'bargain' suit Ma had obtained for Llewellyn had brought too many sleepless nights for him to be able to ignore the consequences of folly. 'Can't you just imagine the scene if they got as far as a job interview?'

Rafferty grabbed Llewellyn's file of papers, adopted a nose-in-the-air manner and intoned, 'I see your last firm was Watts and Cutley. Tell me, Mr/Mrs/Ms Blank, did you leave there suddenly? Only I notice you can't have had another job to go to as you've been unemployed since you left.'

Handing Llewellyn back his file, he said, 'See? Even if they omitted to mention the industrial tribunal on the application form, they'd be bound to put the facts of their employment down; their P45 would reveal it if they didn't. Employers always want details of your last employer. Can't you just imagine what Barstaple or the bosses at Watts and Cutley would tell any prospective employer who contacted them?'

Llewellyn stood his ground. 'There are laws against giving unfair references, you know and—'

'Try proving someone's lied about you when the real reference is given over the phone. By the time Barstaple had finished, no employer would touch you with a pro-tectively clothed barge-pole. Mr Gallagher's right. Stick up for yourself by going to a tribunal and you're branded a troublemaker; the bosses know it, the workers – those with any sense – know it, even what remains of the trade union's muscle know it. Though there's always a few brave souls who go for it. Even if their old firm's forced to take them back it's likely to be what you'd call a – a pyr—' Frustrated in his inability to recall the precise word, Rafferty stumbled to a halt. Llewellyn supplied it.

'Pyrrhic victory?'

'Exactly.'

Now Gallagher added his two-pennyworth. 'The inspector's right. Employment-protection laws can only protect you so far. In reality, if you work for a firm determined to get you out you'd need to be a real tough cookie to either cling on or fight. I could tell you a few tales from the States that would give you goosebumps. I guess Clive Barstaple took lessons from a master. For sure, he knew more than one way to skin a rabbit, more than one way to encourage staff to de-hire themselves. From a caring, family firm, this place has become hell on earth in a few short months. Most of us have been clinging to the cliff like reluctant lemmings, waiting for Barstaple to ice us.'

Surprised that Gallagher should be so frank in the circumstances, Rafferty observed, 'And now somebody's iced him.'

'Couldn't happen to a more deserving guy.'

Gallagher had been very informative. Rafferty wondered why. He thought it interesting that he should also confirm that Barstaple had worked late fairly often. Certainly, he had stayed at the office at least once a week till getting on for seven o'clock. It was a direct contradiction of Ada Collins' evidence. Of course, she had said she usually cleaned the ground floor, so it was possible she had never encountered him. Still, it was curious and he made a mental note to look further into it.

Rafferty left Gallagher and Llewellyn in the empty office to await the arrival of Alistair Plumley and returned upstairs. The scenes of crime team were still busy.

As though drawn by an invisible magnet, Rafferty found himself standing in the doorway of Barstaple's office. He closed his eyes, forced himself to ignore the still-lingering odours as well as the idle comments of the SOCOs, and let the atmosphere of the place seep into him.

Even now, though the coroner's officer had authorized the removal of Barstaple's body, Rafferty could feel the man's presence. He didn't need to read again the many management-speak communications that were pinned to the general noticeboard – each signed by the dead man – to realize that Barstaple had been a tyrant. The evidence had been there in the dead man's mean little mouth, the close-set eyes, the imperious thrust of the nose: mean, devious, proud – what a combination. No wonder somebody had killed him.

The shame of it was that added to these lesser qualities must have been a marked intelligence, as well as sufficient courage to set himself up as a freelance. The pity was he had used these attributes to assist asset-stripping bosses. Surely, he thought, he could have found something more worthy to which to apply his talents?

But then he recalled what Hal Gallagher had said. From that, it sounded as if Barstaple had taken a real pride in his work. It was incomprehensible to Rafferty that anyone could take pride in making other people's lives miserable. Had it never occurred to the man that one of his victims might just turn nasty?

'Vengeance is mine, sayeth the Lord. I will repay,' he muttered, as the voice of his old Religious Instruction teacher echoed back down the years.

'Not if someone beats Him to it, it's not,' one of the SOCO team commented.

Rafferty nodded, smiled an acknowledgement and turned away. It looked like somebody had done just that.

Four

So far, Rafferty and Llewellyn had only had the opportunity for a cursory inspection of the premises. Now, Rafferty returned downstairs and collected Llewellyn. Before Watts and Cutley's 'big cheese', Alistair Plumley, arrived he wanted them to have the grand tour.

Aimhurst and Son's offices stood twenty yards or so back from the road, with parking places for ten cars in front. The grounds incorporated a roadway that led right round the premises. Obviously, the building had originally been a quite substantial residence. Victorian in its heavy use of the ornate, it must have been gutted and turned into offices before the protecting hand of the architectural environmentalists held sway.

Rafferty thought it a pity; he loved the gloriously robust individuality of such buildings, convinced that only soul-less designers could come up with the uninspiring functionalism of most modern architecture. After the attentions of the architects with no souls, the building had become a sad hybrid and, to Rafferty's fanciful imagination, it seemed aware of it. Dwarfed by its high-rise concrete neighbours, its grandeur compromised to commerce and its facade grubby, its roofline seemed bowed in dejection.

Feeling that, so far, everything today seemed designed to depress him, Rafferty forced himself into a more businesslike frame of mind. 'Come on,' he said to

Llewellyn. 'Let's get on with it.' At a brisk pace, he headed round the side of the building. It had two entrances, one at the front and one at the rear. The rear entrance had a sturdy, cinema-style door that could only be opened from the inside.

'These'll have to be checked thoroughly,' Rafferty commented as they passed two commercial-sized refuse containers that stood just past the back door.

Llewellyn nodded.

Although he now knew that the much larger firm of Watts and Cutley had recently taken Aimhurst's over, Rafferty was surprised at the extent of the security. Apart from burglar alarms with the usual infrared sensors, the security stretched to floodlights that would illuminate all round the building as well as a key-numbering system on the front door that the staff used to gain access when the security guard wasn't at his post. It all seemed a bit over the top for such a small concern, especially as the premises held only offices. Aimhurst's were wholesalers, their customers would be other businesses rather than the general public, their receipts crossed cheques or credit transfers rather than cash. Admittedly, they had expensive computer equipment, but even so . . . He glanced at Llewellyn. 'Inside job, you reckon?'

Llewellyn nodded. 'Almost certainly, given the level of security.' He paused, then added, 'Though, of course, as the victim was poisoned rather than shot or stabbed or killed by other more immediate physical means, it's possible someone from outside could have administered the poison via the victim's brought-in lunch.'

'Vengeful wife or girlfriend, you mean, hoping to shift suspicion?'

Llewellyn nodded. 'Poisoning is usually regarded as a woman's crime,' he pointed out.

It certainly seemed reasonable to believe the poison had been in the prawns, Rafferty reflected. And whether they had been doctored at home or in the office, suspicion had certainly been well spread. According to Hal Gallagher, they had been defrosting on a plate in the Aimhurst staff kitchen all morning, available for anyone to tamper with.

'You'd have thought he'd have had the wit not to leave himself so wide open to revenge,' said Rafferty. 'After all, he might have been reckoned a bastard, but, by all accounts, he was a clever one.'

'It's surprising how often men like Barstaple ignore elementary precautions,' said Llewellyn. 'And arrogance of that stamp has a tendency to bring about its own downfall.' After casting an oblique glance at Rafferty, he added softly, 'The ancient Romans had a saying that I think would cover it.'

'There's a novelty,' Rafferty murmured.

'"*Arte perire sua*" – to perish by one's own machinations would be a literal translation. Certainly, it may well turn out that Clive Barstaple's machinations were the death of him. Of course, it's very difficult to make oneself totally secure from poison.'

Rafferty nodded and threw up a quote of his own before he realized what he was doing. '"No man is an island complete of himself." Bloody hell. Your habit of borrowing homilies is catching. Whose bit of borrowed wisdom was that, anyway?'

'John Donne's,' said Llewellyn. 'From his "Meditations".' Loftily, he added, 'And if you're going to borrow from Donne, might I suggest you use the correct version. It's "No man is an Island, entire of it self." '

'Pardon my ignorance.' Know-all git, thought Rafferty. 'Though whichever way you say it, the man had a point.

46

Barstaple the Bastard obviously disregarded the fact that human islands bump against one another continuously. He must have thought his particular island was immune from life's storms.'

They turned the corner and headed round the far side of the building. The rain had fallen off to a thin drizzle and, as the clouds parted, Rafferty saw that, all the time, a full moon had been lurking behind them. Madman's moon, his ma called it. He shivered and hoped it wasn't an omen. Hadn't the notorious poisoner Graham Young started his killings in an office environment?

Rafferty shook himself and told himself not to be ridiculous. Barstaple's murder had been a sane enough act, most likely committed by someone pushed beyond endurance. Rafferty, given his current difficulty concerning Llewellyn's wedding suit and its possible effect on his own career, felt a most unpolicemanlike empathy for such a final solution and its practitioner.

They turned the last corner and returned to the front of the building. Rafferty, thinking of human islands again, murmured to himself, 'Perhaps, just before he died, Barstaple's island saw its own vulnerability. Shame it came too late.'

They returned inside. Alistair Plumley, Hal Gallagher's 'big cheese' boss, arrived five minutes later. He'd evidently been attending either a function or a very posh dinner party, because he wore a dicky bow and dinner jacket. He even sported a scarlet cummerbund and looked a very important island indeed; one with an isthmus, no less, Rafferty thought. If he was to accommodate both his professional and personal egos he would certainly need the extra space, he mused as he sized Plumley up.

Plumley was around thirty-six, Rafferty guessed, as

47

they shook hands. And although his waistline was beginning to spread, mentally he seemed tough. Tall, around 6′ 2″, he carried the extra pounds with ease. The jawline was firm, the gaze a self-assured battleship grey. Rafferty had no trouble guessing he'd be a difficult customer to tangle with. Hopefully, no tangling would be necessary.

'Sorry you've been dragged away from your dinner, sir,' Rafferty began as he led Plumley and Llewellyn into the now empty staff room.

'Not your fault, Inspector,' Plumley had the grace to concede. 'Bloody awful do, anyway. Charity dinner, with the usual plastic food and inferior wine. I was glad to get away.' His brief smile hovered between them and for the first time Rafferty got a glimpse of the charm concealed beneath the steel.

Plumley must suddenly have recalled the reason for his abrupt calling away because he smothered his gaffe with another brief smile and the charm washed over them again. 'Not that I wouldn't rather have endured it than be called away under such circumstances. Poor Clive.' The steel overlaid the charm as he fixed Rafferty with an uncompromising gaze. 'Heart attack, was it?'

'No, sir. I'm afraid not.' Rafferty paused before he added, 'It would appear that Mr Barstaple ate something that disagreed with him. In short, we believe he was murdered.'

Plumley stared hard at him for a few seconds. 'I see. And he was murdered here, where he worked.' His gaze clouded over and Rafferty wondered if he was mentally calculating the commercial implications of Barstaple's death.

However, it seemed he'd misjudged the man, for now Plumley commented quietly, 'He was my placeman. He did my bidding. I hope the fact that he died here is just an unhappy coincidence. I would feel morally responsible should it turn out that his work here brought his death. I hope he didn't suffer.'

'I'm afraid it wasn't an easy death, sir. Poison seldom is.'

'Poison?' Plumley's lips thinned. 'Gallagher didn't mention—'

'He didn't know, sir.' Rafferty felt obliged to save the engaging Gallagher from any possible repercussions. 'I understand he tried to contact you straight after my sergeant here,' he gestured to the silent Llewellyn, 'phoned him to advise him of Mr Barstaple's death. I imagine he felt he had to let you know the little he knew as soon as possible.'

'Yes. Of course. I see. Where is Gallagher now? He's still here, I take it?'

Rafferty nodded. After he'd questioned them, he had let the cleaners go home, but Hal Gallagher, by mutual consent, had remained on the premises.

Alistair Plumley made for the door. 'I want to see him.'

'In a moment, sir.'

Plumley turned, evidently not best pleased at the delay. 'What is it, Inspector? Whatever it is, surely it can wait. I need to speak—'

'This will only take a few minutes, sir. There are a few things I'd like to get clear in my mind. For instance, Mr Barstaple – what did you know about him? I gather he's a self-employed consultant and that you hired him as an interim manager?'

Plumley evidently didn't feel the need to confirm this. 'Obviously Gallagher's told you all this? I can't—'

'Please, sir. As you said, Clive Barstaple was your man. Your responsibility and—'

Plumley winced at this. 'You've made your point,

Inspector. You know what he was doing here. What else do you want to know?'

'Was he liked?' Although Rafferty already knew the answer to that, he wanted to hear how Plumley would respond.

Plumley raised thick dark eyebrows. 'What do you think, Inspector? Pretty unlikely in the circumstances, wouldn't you say? I'm sure you've been told that Clive Barstaple had been hired to wield the axe, something which seems unfortunately to have become common knowledge around here. To answer your question, no, of course he wasn't liked. I didn't employ him to become Mr Popularity. I wanted a job done and I judged him the most competent to do it. He had a reputation for getting results, which is why I hired him.'

Plumley seemed to feel the need to add more. 'To be blunt, Inspector, Watts and Cutley didn't buy this firm to add Aimhurst's staff to the payroll . . . We wanted the Aimhurst Widget amongst other things, and that's all. It's just business. We do have shareholders to answer to.'

Plumley and business types of his ilk certainly didn't answer to their consciences, Rafferty thought. He doubted Plumley had a conscience. Or if he had, it certainly wasn't of the censorious Catholic variety. Rafferty's gave him almost as much trouble as his selectively law-abiding family.

Not for the first time, he reflected than an active Catholic conscience was the best curb on a man's behaviour he'd ever come across. It was a pity the courts couldn't dish them out instead of fines and prison sentences. He was convinced they would be much more effective at reducing the crime statistics. He supposed that a businessman like Alistair Plumley would assume that 'just business' was not only adequate explanation but also sufficient excuse. Now he commented, 'I don't suppose the staff saw it that way. I gather some of them have been here for years, felt part of a family.'

Plumley gave a faint sigh. 'Look, Inspector, Robert Aimhurst was into paternalism, I'm not. Neither was his son or he wouldn't have accepted my offer. Now was there anything else you wanted to know or do you expect me to stand here the rest of the night justifying my business methods?'

Llewellyn broke into the suddenly hostile atmosphere. 'How many of the staff were to go? All of them?'

'No. Every firm has a few key workers who are worth their weight in gold. It was part of Barstaple's brief to appraise the employees here and see if any were of interest to us. As a matter of fact, he was due to bring the interim report on his recommendations to my office tomorrow morning.'

Rafferty wondered why Gallagher hadn't mentioned this report. He seemed a well-informed man and was likely to have been aware of it. 'And have you any idea what this report contained? For instance, who, exactly, did Barstaple suggest was surplus to requirements?'

Plumley grimaced at his choice of phrase. 'I have no idea. I'm sure you can appreciate that my firm has wide-ranging interests. I can't oversee every tiny detail. That's the reason I hire people like Barstaple. He came highly recommended from the last company that made use of his services.'

'And they were?'

Plumley named a firm that Rafferty had never heard of.

'Small, but prestigious,' was Plumley's comment. 'Their head office is in north London.'

Rafferty nodded as Llewellyn noted the details. 'This

51

report – you said he was to bring it to you rather than post it?'

'That's right. Obviously I'd want to discuss the details with him. Why do you ask?'

'It's just that we haven't found such a document in his office. Of course, it's possible he was working on it at his home.'

'Probably hadn't printed it out yet. I believe he worked a lot on his lap-top so I imagine it would be on that.'

Rafferty nodded. There had been no lap-top computer in Barstaple's office. He could only hope they found it at his home. 'I understand Mr Barstaple had only worked here for three months?'

Plumley nodded. 'That's correct. He joined us at the end of November on a six-month contract.'

'Not a very long time in which to make an enemy who wants you dead, and dead in such an awful way,' Rafferty mused.

Plumley seemed to guess his thoughts. After his first shocked concern that his demands might bring a certain moral responsibility for Barstaple's death, he now swiftly backtracked. 'I wouldn't jump to conclusions, if I were you, Inspector. Thinking about it, it's unlikely that one of the staff here killed him. They had no reason to. He was merely a tool. With or without Clive Barstaple's undoubted skills, heads were going to roll. As far as the staff here are concerned his death alters nothing. Unless old man Aimhurst employed idiots – and that wouldn't altogether surprise me – the staff would have known that. From their point of view, Barstaple's death accomplishes nothing.'

'Reason doesn't always enter into it, sir,' he commented. Besides, thought Rafferty, as he'd already discussed with Llewellyn, given the level of security it seemed unlikely an outsider could have gained access. 'I take it you change the access code on the entrance keying system regularly?'

From the quick narrowing of Plumley's gaze he evidently saw where this was leading, but was forced to admit that he didn't know. 'You'd have to ask Hal Gallagher. As I said, I don't deal with such day-to-day matters. But it seems likely. It would be imprudent to allow any ex-employee with a grudge to gain access, after all.'

So unless the murder was connected to his private life, it seemed to Rafferty even more likely his work here led to his death. 'Tell me, was he married or—?'

'I've no idea. I didn't enquire into his love life when I hired him.' Plumley's lips drew together as he went on, and although it was with evident reluctance that he heaped more suspicion on the staff, he was honest enough to add, 'Though I would suspect not. Somehow he didn't strike me as the marrying kind.' He paused and looked thoughtfully at Rafferty. 'There's another aspect you ought to be aware of. Since the takeover, Aimhurst and Son have received some threats. They gave no names, of course, but to judge from the subject matter, I'd guess they were from animal-rights activists.

'Watts and Cutley, amongst other things, have a pharmaceutical arm where we use animals in laboratory tests. I suppose, after the takeover, these animal-rights people thought this place would be an easy target. We updated the security system because of their threats. Maybe you should look into their activities?'

'We'll certainly do that, sir,' Rafferty agreed. 'I imagine Mr Gallagher has the details?'

Plumley nodded. 'If that's all, Inspector . . . ?'

'For the moment. Now, you wanted a word with Mr

Gallagher. Llewellyn, perhaps you'd escort Mr Plumley to the other office?'

As Plumley followed Llewellyn out, Rafferty watched him. Although Plumley had managed to spread a little of the guilt outwards from the firm with his revelations about the animal-rights activists' threats, the man struck him as a realist. He would realize as well as Rafferty that, apart from the difficulty an outsider would have in gaining access, the method of murder indicated a knowledge of the victim's habits, which only an intimate was likely to possess.

It was apparent the realization didn't please Alistair Plumley. But he hadn't wasted his time in futile denial. Instead, just before he followed Llewellyn, his gaze had once more become shuttered and Rafferty guessed he was planning his damage-limitation exercise. He was curious to know how Alistair Plumley hoped to turn the murderer's woeful lack of team spirit to the company's advantage.

Five

R afferty was in his office early on Thursday. He had asked Hal Gallagher for the personnel files and he wanted to go through them, learn something of the staff before he spoke to them later in the morning.

Apart from the files of the firm's current staff, he had also obtained those of the staff who had left between the death of Robert Aimhurst and the murder of Clive Barstaple. He was thankful there had been no more than three such departures, thankful, too, that, having reached the superstitiously significant figure of three deaths they must now have reached the week's total cadaver tally. It was a comforting thought and one he confided to Llewellyn as he arrived with the canteen tea. 'I know that with its two corpses, yesterday was decidedly gutty, but let's look on the bright side. We're three corpses up and should be safe from any more – for this week at least.'

As the Welshman didn't share his superstitious beliefs, Rafferty was surprised when, after putting the tea down on the desk, Llewellyn nodded and remarked, 'Yesterday was a Dismal Day, so—'

'You can say that again,' Rafferty broke in and waved at his office window and the sodden grey sky. 'And, weather-wise at least, it doesn't look as if today's going to be any better. February – the dreariest month of the year.

55

Ma reckons her daffodil bulbs have rotted.' He scowled. 'Bloody weather.'

'I was actually referring to yesterday's date,' Llewellyn told him, 'not its events or the weather. The 26th of February is one of the so-called Dismal Days of the year. Each month has two, traditionally regarded as evil or unlucky days. Comes from the Latin *"Dies mali"*.'

'Might have known you'd drag those ancient Romans in somehow,' said Rafferty. 'It was certainly a dismal day for Clive Barstaple,' he added, in an attempt to deflect Llewellyn from sounding off on his favourite topic. It was a forlorn hope. Llewellyn had connected with the part of his brain where he stored such edifying titbits and was not to be diverted from sharing the benefits of a superior education with Rafferty.

'If my memory serves me correctly,' he said, 'they're also known as Egyptian Days; though there are two views on why that should be so. Some say they had been computed by Egyptian astrologers, others say they were connected with the plagues of Egypt.'

Rafferty forced a smile as grey as the day. 'I wonder what view our esteemed cadaver would favour? It certainly sounds as if Clive Barstaple was a past master at making plagues of enemies.'

He sat on the edge of his desk, dislodging the pile of staff files which began to totter. Llewellyn rescued them as Rafferty expanded. 'From what Hal Gallagher said, Barstaple had succeeded in persuading some of the staff at Aimhurst and Son to leave. Without redundancy pay, of course. The rest, he'd apparently intimidated and browbeaten to such an extent they must have been on the verge of doing likewise. Barstaple seems to have been a thoroughly nasty piece of work. Who could blame them if one of them decided to rationalize him?'

'"*Oderint dum metuant*".' Llewellyn was off again. 'Let them hate, provided they fear,' he translated. 'A method of man-management attributed to the Emperor Tiberius. In this case, of course, it must have suited Barstaple's brief very well. A frightened workforce is not usually the most efficient, which would have given him the excuse he needed to dispense with their services.'

Rafferty nodded. 'Dangerous balancing act, though – keeping the fear greater than the hate. Get it wrong and puff, you're dead, as this particular exponent of the bully-boy school of business ethics discovered. Still,' he frowned, 'Plumley was right about one thing. If Watts and Cutley were determined to wriggle out of their commitment to keep Aimhurst's staff on the payroll they'd have only taken some other rationalization expert on to do Barstaple's job. Whoever killed him must have realized that.'

'You said yourself that reason doesn't always enter into it. After weeks of stress, worry and insecurity their hatred would naturally have focused on Barstaple himself. After all, he was the one making their lives miserable.'

Rafferty nodded. 'You know, I've been congratulating myself that our line-up of suspects is naturally limited to current staff at Aimhurst's, the recently fired, and anyone he was intimate with in his personal life. But I don't reckon we're going to be that lucky.'

Obligingly, Llewellyn quirked an enquiring eyebrow. 'What do you mean?'

'Simply this. We know visitors to the premises have to sign in, but who – exactly – would be regarded as visitors? I doubt other employees in the group at large would bother with such a formality. And another thing – maybe Barstaple wasn't the only person to have changed jobs recently. What I mean is, maybe someone from his

57

past – someone with a grudge against him – also changed jobs. Barstaple was, by all accounts, very successful at what he did and Watts and Cutley has quite a number of subsidiaries. Sounds to me like there could be a fair number of people with reason to hate Barstaple. I wonder what would be the chances of one of them ending up at one of those subsidiaries? We daren't ignore the possibility.'

Llewellyn's less emotional temperament took the fact in his stride. 'But it should be easy enough to find out. We've got the details of Barstaple's previous consultancy appointments, do you want me to get on to their personnel managers and ask for the details of the relevant staff?'

Rafferty nodded. 'It may be a long shot, but it's worth a try. After all, nasty pieces of work like Barstaple don't become nasty overnight.'

Llewellyn nodded. 'Juvenal said something similar in his *Satires*.'

'Smart bloke, old Juvenal,' Rafferty broke in quickly before Llewellyn could get launched on another erudite quotation. 'Talk about great minds thinking alike, hey?' Llewellyn made no comment as to the greatness of Rafferty's mind. Instead, he said, 'I'll make a start on checking with the other firms for whom Barstaple worked as a consultant.' He paused. 'I imagine you'll want someone put on to investigating the animal-rights angle?'

'It'll probably be another dead end, but like the previous victims of his rationalizing, it's got to be checked out. Ring Plumley and Gallagher. Find out what form this threat took – if it was a letter and they still have it, ask for it.' He walked round the desk, sat down and dragged the pile of staff files towards him. 'While you do that, I'll plough on with these.'

*   *   *

Dr Sam Dally rang with the results of the post-mortem five minutes after Llewellyn left the office.

'What have you got for me, Sam?' Rafferty asked when Dally was put through.

'As your resident expert guessed, the victim died of carbohydrate andromedotoxin, which the rhododendron and mountain laurels both contain. A highly toxic substance. All parts of the plant are poisonous, by the way. Pretty plants and pretty women, Rafferty, both can be lethal to a man.'

'Ain't that the truth.' Rafferty pursed his lips thoughtfully. Llewellyn had questioned Eric Penn again and discovered that Eric had washed Barstaple's lunch dishes on Wednesday evening, a fact which had concentrated Rafferty's suspicions. 'Barstaple ate prawns for lunch yesterday,' he told Sam. 'I suppose the poison was on them?'

'You suppose wrong, Rafferty. Doesn't the law say "innocent until proven guilty"? I imagine that applies to prawns as well.'

Rafferty took Sam's light rebuke with good grace. Unfortunately, he had never overcome his tendency to jump to conclusions so he had plenty of practice in having his nose rubbed in his mistakes.

'Anyway, these prawns were innocent,' Sam went on. 'It was the yoghurt that killed him – or rather, what was in the yoghurt. I'd guess someone put the plant in a blender and either injected the resulting liquid toxin with a syringe or cut a small hole in the bottom of the yoghurt pot, spooned it in and sealed it with a little bit of sticky tape. Unlikely the victim would turn the pot upside-down and discover it.'

Good grace notwithstanding, Rafferty wasn't above getting pleasure out of contradicting Sam and now he told him, 'There was no hole in the pot that was in Barstaple's wastebin. Not even a tiny one such as a syringe would make.'

'Was there not?' Sam paused, obviously searching for something to confound Rafferty's evidence. As usual, he succeeded. 'What flavour was the yoghurt in the bin?'

'Hazelnut flavour.'

'That explains it.' Sam sounded smug. 'I don't know what that was doing in the bin, but I do know that whoever ate it, it wasn't the victim. Apart from coffee, he'd only eaten the prawns and a strawberry yoghurt. The poison was in that.'

Rafferty just managed to stop himself from asking who, then, had eaten the hazelnut yoghurt. He asked another stupid question instead, the idiocy of which he realized too late. 'Wouldn't he have tasted the poison?' Obviously not, was the answer. He wouldn't have eaten more than a spoonful of it if so, a fact which Dally was quick to confirm.

'Carbohydrate andromedotoxin doesn't have a strong flavour. Anyway, as I've already told you, it would need only a tiny amount to kill, no more than a five-mil spoonful.'

'What about shelf-life?' Rafferty questioned. 'We don't know when the poison was put in the pot of yoghurt, but would its effectiveness have been greatly reduced over time?'

'As to that, I'd have to check, but as the victim's dead, the poison's potency lasted long enough to do its job so it hardly matters. It should be a simple enough matter to find out when that yoghurt was bought – when you've done that you'll also discover the earliest time the poison could have been added to it.'

Rafferty grunted an acknowledgement of this, then

remarked wistfully, 'Pity the poison wasn't in the prawns. According to the deputy manager, Barstaple brought them in on the morning of his death, so they were only in the kitchen for a few hours. It's something I've yet to check out, but I'd guess the yoghurt cartons were there since at least the Monday as there was only one left in the fridge when we arrived and most people buy packs of four or six at a time. If so, they'd have been there for anyone to tamper with for several days, which makes things considerably more tricky.'

'I suppose you've considered the possibility that it wasn't necessarily Barstaple's yoghurt that was poisoned?'

'What do you mean?' Rafferty frowned. He hadn't thought much about the yoghurt at all, truth to tell. More fool him, he realized, as Sam went on.

'Always supposing his would-be poisoner had access to the office fridge, all this poisoner would need to do was to note the manufacturer and flavours of yoghurt that Barstaple had bought and then buy the same. That way, his killer could put the poison in at their leisure at home. It would be only a matter of seconds to switch Barstaple's original pot of yoghurt for its poisoned twin.'

Rafferty didn't like Sam's conclusions. If what he outlined had actually happened it was going to make pinning Barstaple's murderer down that much more difficult. 'You're absolutely sure the poison was in the yoghurt?' he asked, desperate to debunk Sam's theory. It was an unwise move. 'I'd have thought—'

'In this instance I'm the one paid to do the thinking,' Sam crisply reminded him. 'And I'm telling you I'm sure.'

Rafferty had to accept it, but as consolation, he had now come up with a theory about the hazelnut yoghurt.

'Anyway, no matter who brought the poisoned yoghurt into the office, it's obvious that someone deliberately removed the empty, poisoned yoghurt carton from the bin, emptied the hazelnut one of its contents – presumably down the sink in the kitchen – and then placed it in Barstaple's wastebin. The thing I want to know is why? What possible advantage did the killer think they'd get from it?'

'I've no idea, Rafferty. But I suggest we make a pact. You don't try to tell me my job and I won't try to tell you yours.'

As he'd already, most effectively too, told Rafferty his job, this suggested pact would put Rafferty at a severe disadvantage, so he demurred, adding, 'But thanks for the offer, Sam. You're all heart.'

'I know. And that being the case, I'll tell you one thing that occurred to me. It's my guess your poisoner assumed the prawns and yoghurt would get so jumbled together in the victim's stomach we wouldn't be able to tell precisely where the poison was introduced, especially without the help of an obviously poisoned yoghurt pot. The poisoner probably hoped we'd concentrate on the prawns and whoever had the opportunity to tamper with them yesterday. If he – or she – was lucky and deliberately out of the office on the day he died, they might expect to be removed from the list of suspects altogether.'

'And would you say that was a reasonable expectation for the killer to have?'

'Reasonable enough for a layman. As long as the victim ate the yoghurt immediately after the prawns.'

Rafferty brightened. At least they could check who had been out of the office yesterday. It might give them a helpful pointer. 'Thanks, Sam. You've certainly given me plenty of food for thought.'

'Well, while you're chewing on it, a word of advice.'
'What's that?'
'Don't eat the yoghurt.'

When Llewellyn returned to the office after getting in touch with Barstaple's previous firms, Rafferty told him Dally's post-mortem findings. 'Sam suggested the killer was probably hoping to confuse the issue by putting the poison in the yoghurt rather than Barstaple's main lunch dish. What do you think?'

'It's something to be considered,' replied Llewellyn with his usual caution. 'It's possible, of course, as Dr Dally inferred, that the person who poisoned him wasn't in the office yesterday. Equally, it could be that whoever killed him just wanted to spread suspicion by making it look as if the poison could have been introduced to the food on another day. On similar lines, maybe the location of the murder was chosen to confuse. Was he killed in his office because his murderer either didn't know where he lived or was unable to gain access? Or because, for the killer, the location of the murder held symbolic significance?'

Rafferty sighed. 'Don't go getting all psychological on me,' he pleaded. 'At least, not this early in the case.' He'd already overdosed on ancient Greeks and Romans. The last thing he wanted was the not-so-ancient Freud and Niesc – Nits – whatever his name was – getting in on the act.

Ignoring the interruption, Llewellyn went on. 'Then again, for all we know, we're crediting the killer with more intelligence than they possess. Maybe they just put the poison into whatever food was available at a time they were available to administer it and were prepared to await results.'

'Light blue touchpaper and retire, hey?' Rafferty grinned. 'But if that's the case, why not wait for a more convenient time and a wider choice of foodstuffs in which to put the poison? It would have the advantage of spreading suspicion, too.'

Llewellyn shrugged. 'I doubt they'd have chosen to put the poison on the prawns, anyway. Barstaple would surely have noticed if the prawns suddenly gained a sauce, however minute.'

'I suppose so.'

'We've so far more or less assumed that it was one of Barstaple's colleagues who killed him. But we ought to give more consideration to the possibility that someone unconnected with his work hated him and that, as Dr Dally suggested, the victim brought in yoghurt that had already been poisoned. Such a killer could have found a willing accomplice in the office to swap the pots in the wastebin. We mustn't forget that we're talking about a man with a strong talent for making enemies. Maybe he made use of his "let them hate, provided they fear" philosophy at home, too.'

Rafferty shook his head. 'Maybe he would have done,' he said. 'But, luckily for us, he didn't have anyone at home.' He had already instigated inquiries about Barstaple's living arrangements. Unfortunately, the neighbours had known little about him. There had been no sign of a wife or other live-in partner at Barstaple's home. Of course, he might have had some more casual arrangement which would reveal itself in due course – but a casual lover was unlikely to be a killing kind of lover, certainly not of the premeditated kind as Barstaple's killer had been.

The search of Barstaple's home had failed to find his lap-top computer. Rafferty made a mental note to question Aimhurst's staff about it; if he had been using it at his office on the day of his murder *someone* would surely have noticed.

Tired yesterday evening, he hadn't noticed the loose sheet of paper tucked between the personnel files, so Llewellyn hadn't had the opportunity to learn more about the victim. But now Rafferty handed him the PR puff about Barstaple's business consultancy service, which Gallagher must have thought they'd find helpful. Pity he hadn't mentioned it at the time, Rafferty had thought when he found it.

In it, along with his educational background and qualifications, Barstaple had boasted of being a bachelor, having no ties, no wife or child to make demands on him.

Rafferty thought it strange that Alistair Plumley hadn't been aware of the fact. But then, he reasoned, Plumley hadn't struck him as a man to be overly concerned with the workers' private lives, certainly not when the worker in question was a hired consultant like Barstaple.

Barstaple's handout displayed no false modesty when it went on to proclaim that, as he was only twenty-eight, his energy was considerable and he would be able to devote it all to his work.

As Llewellyn handed back the PR puff, Rafferty added, 'Of course, he could have lied about his marital status, simply to make himself look an even more attractive proposition to potential clients. But, until we can check further, we'll take him at his word that he's not only currently single, but hasn't even got a messy divorce in his recent past. Which, if confirmed, will make our job a little easier, particularly as you remarked that poisoning is most often thought of as a woman's crime.' He paused for a moment. 'To get back to the yoghurts. We'll have to check out where and when he bought them and when he brought them into the office. Even if Sam's right and someone bought identical yoghurt and added the poison at their leisure, it doesn't really matter for our purposes. If, for the moment, we discount the possibility of an accomplice, it's who had the opportunity to swap the yoghurts in the wastebin that will lead us to our murderer.'

Rafferty glanced down at Barstaple's PR puff. It said he had left university seven years earlier after following a business studies course. He'd come out of it with Honours. 'Must have been the last time Barstaple came out of anything with honours,' he commented as he tapped the relevant section.

Barstaple had provided Watts and Cutley with glowing testimonials from half a dozen previous clients and, to judge from what Alistair Plumley had said, was evidently regarded as a high-flyer, a term Rafferty viewed with distaste. In his experience, high-flyers were often people who would do anything to get ahead. The term always made him wonder about the poor sods such high-flyers used as a launch pad.

Since finding the PR puff, Rafferty had made a few inquiries and discovered that Barstaple had set himself up two years previously as a consultant, a troubleshooter, an expert who hired himself out to firms who wished to rationalize. It was a business he ran from home. He had obviously excelled at the role as he had gone from strength to strength. Of course, the times they lived in meant Barstaple's particular expertise was in demand. Firms were being rationalized, people de-hired all over the place.

Rafferty shivered as a stout policeman who bore more than a passing resemblance to Superintendent Bradley walked over his grave. If Bradley discovered the real provenance of Llewellyn's wedding suit, being de-hired was the least he could expect. With a determined shrug, he dismissed the thought and turned back to the matter in hand.

After filling Llewellyn in on the rest of his discoveries, Rafferty returned to the Welshman's earlier comment. 'Of course, it's possible Barstaple crossed swords with a neighbour.' He grinned, 'Or maybe he picked a fight with the milkman over the bill.' He had been more than half-joking about the latter, but now he added, 'That's a thought. Barstaple didn't live far from Aimhurst's offices. It might be an idea to find out if the same milkman delivers there as delivers in the neighbourhood of his home.'

In an attempt to divert his mind from the many problems besetting it, Rafferty joked, 'What a turn-up it would be if our vengeful killer turned out to be his friendly neighbourhood milkman, clutching a pint of gold top in one hand and a poisoned carton of yoghurt in the other.'

It was pretty unlikely, Rafferty admitted to himself. Still, if they failed to find a receipt for the yoghurt's purchase, that could explain the reason why. If Barstaple's milkman was anything like Rafferty's, his bills would be masterpieces of brevity and consist of nothing more than the date and a total amount due written in bold strokes that discouraged argument.

'One point about your murdering milkman, sir.'

'What's that?'

'He might be in an ideal position to poison the yoghurt, but would he be able to swap cartons and remove the poisoned one from Barstaple's office?'

'Possibly, if our poisoning milkman had an accomplice as you assumed a murdering lover might have. Let's face it, our victim seems the kind of man who would cause the most unlikely alliances against him.'

'Anyway, it shouldn't be difficult to find out where he

bought the yoghurt,' said Llewellyn. 'The receipt might still be in his flat.'

Rafferty nodded. 'Better get some more officers round there. I want his place given an even more thorough going-over, not only for that receipt, but also for that rationalization report he was preparing for Alistair Plumley. His lap-top might have gone missing, but there's a fair chance he printed the report out and it's somewhere in his home. Tell Lilley.'

They had already checked the victim's coat pockets and those of the clothes he had been wearing when he died and there had been neither receipt nor report either in them or his desk. Rafferty had left Jonathon Lilley to continue the search at Barstaple's home yesterday evening, but he had so far failed to find either item. 'You've got Barstaple's car keys?'

Llewellyn nodded.

'Make sure the vehicle's checked over as well.' Gallagher had told them it was the Porsche still in the reserved bay at Aimhurst's premises. 'Makes you think, doesn't it?'

'What does, sir?'

'This line the Church peddles about the meek inheriting the earth. Seems to me the only earth the meek inherit is the clods of the stuff that covers their coffins. It's human manure like Clive Barstaple who get the spoils.'

'Much good it did him in the end,' Llewellyn observed.

'Maybe so,' Rafferty murmured. 'But I still wouldn't have minded that Porsche, especially as, if my old religious teacher's to be believed, lapsed Catholics like yours truly aren't reckoned to have much chance of booty in the hereafter either. According to her, I'm more likely to end up getting my bum pricked by the devil's pitchfork for eternity. She was another believer in that adage of yours about letting them hate as long as they fear. The old bat could have given Barstaple lessons.'

Religion was another subject Llewellyn had learned it best to avoid and he maintained a discreet silence until Rafferty returned to the matter in hand.

'One more thing we need to check out is just how tight their security was. I admit it looks pretty impressive, but security is only as good as the human factor providing it. That guard at the desk must pee occasionally, so he presumably leaves the desk unmanned. And we know there's no guard on the premises at night. Did you find out who holds keys to the place?'

Llewellyn nodded. 'Albert Smith, the usual guard from Guardian Security, has one set, as you know. He locks up as soon as the cleaners have finished. The only other people with keys were the victim himself, Gallagher the deputy manager and Alistair Plumley.'

'Right. We'll need to find out if any of those sets of keys were lost or misplaced recently. We also need to find out if there's a spare set and if so, where they're kept. Perhaps you'd get Hanks to look into that while I finish going through these files?'

Llewellyn nodded again and went out.

When Rafferty had finished going through the staff records, he pulled some sheets of paper towards him and started to make a list.

After writing 'Things To Do' in his best writing at the top, he paused, waiting for further inspiration. As usual when it came to paperwork, inspiration was slow in coming and his mind began to wander.

They had yet to find the yoghurt pot containing the poison; he'd had all the rubbish searched as a matter of routine and, although there had been other empty yoghurt pots, a strawberry-flavour one hadn't been amongst them. He frowned as he tried to figure out if there might not be another reason other than the one Sam had suggested for the killer to substitute the poisoned pot for a normal one but he couldn't come up with anything. Probably, it was as Dally had suggested, and that, if it meant anything at all, it was that the killer was merely trying to ensure that the yoghurt was found innocent.

Rafferty gave himself a mental shake, grasped his pen firmly and wrote:

1. Find out who was in the victim's office after, say, one o'clock in the afternoon, by which time, at the earliest, Barstaple would presumably have consumed the yoghurt and discarded the pot in his bin.

2. Of particular relevance to the above, find out if anyone was in Barstaple's office alone at any time that afternoon and had the opportunity to retrieve the poisoned yoghurt pot and substitute it – presumably Barstaple, too, made occasional visits to the lavatory, so was likely to have left his office empty at least once that afternoon.

3. Find out which members of staff were the last to leave on Wednesday evening as the same opportunity as in 2 would have been available to them.

4. Check if any more informal visitors came to the offices that day.

Having made a start, Rafferty sat back. That carton of yoghurt was, he felt, the key to the case. If they could pinpoint who had the opportunity to remove it he was pretty certain they'd find the killer, too. Or at the very least an accomplice.

Pleased with his efforts, Rafferty began on another list; this one of those who were known to have been alone in the victim's office at the relevant times.

At the top he wrote the name of Ada Collins, the contract-cleaning supervisor. Beside her name, he put the word 'unlikely'. She didn't work for Watts and Cutley, so unless she had been one of those rationalized by him in an earlier episode, she had been safe from Barstaple's particular brand of nastiness. Furthermore, she had claimed never to have met the man. Rafferty still considered that unlikely. In his consultancy capacity, Barstaple had been the acting manager, and earned a tidy sum if the brand-new Porsche was anything to go by. He'd hardly pack up dead on five thirty every single evening and, according to both Gallagher and Eric Penn, he hadn't done so.

He made another note against Ada Collins' name, a reminder to check her background, then paused again. Before he sat back, he added the same against the names of the other contract-cleaning staff.

He gazed happily at his neat lists for a few moments, before he remembered they were only a start. And as he thought of all the other checking that lay ahead he slumped in his chair. Maybe it wasn't too late even now to follow his uncles, cousins and brothers into the building trade? Of course, Superintendent Bradley might yet make the decision for him and give him a shove in the direction of such an alternative career – as a trustee in a prison carpentry shop. But Rafferty immediately put that thought aside. Dafyd Llewellyn was a cautious soul, so it was hardly an imminent danger. The wedding suit would hang in the closet for a year or two yet, gathering moths and dust and – with a bit of luck – the label 'unfashionable' to boot. It was a comforting thought and cheered Rafferty immeasurably.

Six

'**B**y the way,' Llewellyn said as they got in the car much later that morning and headed for Aimhurst and Son's offices to interview the staff, 'we were too busy earlier for me to mention it, but Maureen and I have set a date and venue for our wedding.'

Rafferty's hands tightened on the steering wheel. He had congratulated himself too soon. The fates had obviously decided to make an example of him. Llewellyn's news meant the iffy suit had a definite date set for its airing. It explained why Llewellyn had been throwing out so many high-minded quotes. Rafferty had noticed their number went up or down according to whether Llewellyn was happy or miserable.

Still, not to panic, he told himself. Knowing Llewellyn's no-rush mentality, the date was probably months away. He managed to choke out his congratulations.

Llewellyn gave him one of the tiny smiles that were the equivalent of a huge grin from anyone else and confided, 'It was what you said that prompted us.'

Me and my big mouth, thought Rafferty. He prayed he'd get laryngitis next time he felt tempted to give advice against his own best interests. Conscious that his ready tongue had got him into enough trouble already, he managed to avoid giving voice to another of the opinions that were always ready to trip off its tip. Admittedly, it

73

was pretty unromantic to arrange your wedding date right at the start of a murder inquiry, but he was damned if he was going to be the one to say so. He thought he'd said more than enough on the subject of marriage already.

'Yes,' Llewellyn added. 'We've been thinking seriously about it and finally made our minds up. We've compromised on a register office ceremony and will ask our respective churches for blessings afterwards. Maureen had a day off today and went to Elmhurst Register Office to make the arrangements. She rang me just before we left the office to let me know that the date at least is organized.'

Rafferty tried to look pleased at the news. After all, he had been the one to get the romance off the ground. He immediately crunched the gears. To cover his gaffe, he attempted a joke. 'So, when is it? Christmas in the year 2005?' Llewellyn had a well-deserved reputation for caution. Rafferty had relied on it, dammit. 'Remind me to put a note in my five-year diary.'

'It's a little earlier than 2005, actually. It's March. March 29th this year.' Llewellyn paused. 'You know, I haven't been in a Marks and Spencer store for some years. I know they have a reputation for quality, but I didn't realize before that it extended to superior suits at reasonable prices. You should ask your mother to look out for a new one there for you.' Rafferty sensed the pained glance Llewellyn directed at his old brown suit. 'You'll want to look smart for the wedding, especially as Superintendent Bradley's been invited.'

A chilly breeze seemed to flutter around Rafferty's heart at Llewellyn's latest revelation. The fates were really going for the jugular this time. The news about Bradley was all he needed. 'Long-Pockets' Bradley could price anything at a hundred yards, and if Llewellyn wore his iffy suit Bradley would be bound to ask where he'd got it. No way would he be taken in by the fake Marks and Sparks tag. 'Who decided to invite him?'

'Maureen's mother. When Maureen rang her to tell her the news she was so pleased her mother didn't quibble about it being a civil ceremony that she agreed to let her make a start on the invitation list.' Llewellyn directed another of his little smiles at Rafferty. 'I gather Superintendent Bradley was the first name she thought of. She's already dropped his invitation round. She knows him from the Masons' dinner dances. Apparently, Maureen's father's a member.'

I might have known it, Rafferty thought. Maureen's mother, Claire Tyler-Jenkins as was, snob and social climber second to none, would consider it as natural as breathing that, with ambitions to the future, she should invite her prospective son-in-law's big white chief to the wedding. Why didn't that possibility occur to me? he asked himself with dismay. He hadn't exactly endeared himself to the old man and for months Bradley had been looking for a reason to get rid of him. He was unlikely to worry if the means to that end put paid to Llewellyn's career as well as his own.

Absorbed in his plans, Llewellyn rattled on happily, oblivious to the consternation he had caused. Rafferty heard not a word. A heart-thumping panic had blocked most of his senses and his automatic pilot took over the driving. It wasn't difficult for him to imagine the sequence of events after Bradley learned not only of the bargain-basement price of the wedding suit and its claimed and unlikely provenance, but that *his* ma had supplied it. He stifled a groan. The Marks and Sparks label wouldn't fool him for a minute, suspicious-minded git that he was. Somehow Rafferty doubted St Michael would extend his saintly protection under such circumstances. Visions of interrogations, suspension, court rooms and prison chased one another remorselessly across his inner vision; not just for him, but for Llewellyn as well. It would certainly get his and Maureen's marriage off to a flying start.

Preoccupied by this uncomfortable thought, Rafferty turned off the roundabout into Aimhurst and Son's forecourt, parked and got out before the still chatty Llewellyn had time to notice his distracted air.

Constable Smales was on the door, his boyish complexion still green-tinged from his recent post-mortem attendance. Rafferty, at the moment feeling empathy with all the troubled souls in the world – even Smales – spared him a sympathetic glance.

Smales told him that, as he had requested, the employees had been gathered in the ground-floor staff room to await his arrival. Rafferty could, of course, have contacted them the previous evening and told them to stay at home, but he had felt it would be more helpful to the case to get them together on the premises and, hopefully, talking revealingly to one another.

Rafferty nodded at Smales and walked into the reception area. Hal Gallagher was hovering beside WPC Liz Green and immediately he opened the staff-room door for Rafferty to enter.

As soon as he stepped into the room, Rafferty felt the tension in the air. He had warned Hal Gallagher and Albert Smith the security guard to say nothing to the staff about the murder, as he wanted to gauge their reactions when they learned of it. Although he suspected it was too much to hope that the murderer – if he did turn out to be one of the staff – would react in an obvious way, there might just be something.

But if any of the staff harboured an emotion stronger

than curiosity it was well concealed. Of course, with so many police officers on the premises they would be aware that something major had occurred.

As he gazed round at the faces Rafferty could discern nothing more than a heightened excitement at this interesting change to the normal routine, plus an expectation that he was the man who would provide the answers. Nobody looked guilty, fearful or even remorseful. Of course it was reasonable that whoever had killed Barstaple felt no guilt or remorse. After all, if the victim had been a dog he'd have been put down years ago as being too mean-spirited and spiteful.

Apart from Gallagher, all four of the remaining office staff were present and each of them stared at him with varying degrees of curiosity.

'Are you going to tell us what's going on?' a young blonde woman demanded. 'Nobody will tell us anything.' She glanced round at her colleagues and her 'I think we've a right to know,' brought several agreeing nods.

She was an attractive girl with a sensitive oval face, shapely figure and a gleaming bob. Rafferty automatically straightened his shoulders and sucked in what Sam Dally insisted was the beginnings of a paunch. 'I'm sorry,' he said. 'And you are Miss—?'

'Luscombe. Linda Luscombe.

Rafferty flipped open his notebook, but wasn't surprised to discover that he was unable to decipher his scrawled notes.

Llewellyn came to his rescue and extracted the required information from his own notes which he had efficiently and speedily lifted from the staff files before they had left the office. 'Miss Luscombe is here on work experience from the local college, sir.'

Hal Gallagher stepped forward. 'Perhaps I should get

77

the introductions out of the way?' At Rafferty's nod, he worked his way round the room, naming each of the staff. He finished with Rafferty and Llewellyn and introduced them in turn.

Now that the formalities were over the staff stared at him impatiently. 'Right,' said Rafferty. 'I'd better start by telling you why you've all been gathered to wait in your own staff room.' Bluntly, he told them, 'I'm afraid there's been a murder on the premises.'

This produced gasps of astonishment and a certain amount of ghoulish thrill though nothing more suspicious as far as Rafferty could judge. He waited for the excited buzz to die down before adding, 'Mr Clive Barstaple was found dead in his office yesterday evening.'

This shocked them and it was a few seconds before the questions came at him.

'How?'

'Who did it?'

'When exactly?'

Nobody asked why, Rafferty noted.

After the first shocked questions a more wary silence took over. From the covert glances it was clear they were examining motives, opportunities, possible alibis. He guessed the last point might pose them a few problems. As he had already concluded, in this investigation the time of death was of less significance than was usually the case. It was who had had the opportunity to doctor the yoghurt pot, or more importantly, substitute it, that was the question here. He doubted any of them would have an alibi that covered the entire time from its purchase, its placing in the fridge – the timing of both of which they had still to establish – and its consumption, to the substitution of the discarded pot for another.

Linda Luscombe at nineteen had the resilience of youth

78

and recovered far more quickly from the news than her middle-aged colleagues.

'Are we allowed to know how he died?'

Rafferty could see no reason not to tell them. They were likely to find out soon enough from the security guard. 'He was poisoned, Miss Luscombe.'

The colour drained from her face. 'God. I shared Clive's – Mr Barstaple's – lunch yesterday. If it was in that, whoever killed Clive might have murdered me as well.'

Her claim was confirmed by Bob Harris, a grey-faced, worried-looking man of about fifty. 'That's true. They were both eating in his office around twelve thirty. I – I had intended to take my lunch from twelve till one,' he rambled on. 'But Mr Barstaple called me into his office just as I was going for lunch. I was with him till just after twelve thirty and decided not to bother going out after all.'

'Oh, Bob, how upsetting for you.' The woman Hal Gallagher had introduced as Amy Glossop had a thin, embittered face. After her comment, she glanced round at the other members of staff as if looking for approval. Instead, she got stony expressions of dislike. It seemed to spur her on. 'Of course, I left just before noon and didn't realize you weren't able to meet your wife after all. You poor thing.' The sympathetic smile she directed at Harris appeared designed specifically to turn the knife. It certainly made Bob Harris look sick and caused Linda Luscombe to glare at her, a glare that said 'shut up' as clearly as words.

Amy Glossop gave a glance of injured innocence around the room. 'I'm sorry. Have I said something I shouldn't?' The innocence was as patently false as the sympathy. And, as she went artlessly on, sticking the knife in a little deeper, Rafferty wondered what the inoffensive Harris could possibly have done to her.

'It's just that we all know how much yesterday meant to you. I hope Eileen didn't take it too badly.' Amy Glossop turned to Rafferty and explained, 'Bob here had an important date with his estranged wife yesterday lunchtime. Such a shame he had to stand her up.'

Miss Glossop's staff file claimed she was forty-five, Rafferty remembered, but she looked older. And while he thought it possible that someone of Amy Glossop's age could still be naive enough to unwittingly let them know that her colleague had an additional reason to dislike his interim manager, he doubted this was so in her case. There was something about her thin lips and narrowed, bird-bright eyes that told him her comment had been calculated.

It seemed, from their expressions, that the rest of the staff thought so too. He sensed a certain drawing back from the woman. As the room was small this was more mental that physical, but it was obvious that Amy Glossop had noticed it, too. For a moment the veil lifted and raw misery briefly peered out before being as quickly hidden. She hugged herself defensively as though she, rather than Bob Harris, had been the victim here.

Bob Harris looked even sicker than before. On the surface, Harris looked too defeated a man to have the energy to plan his own death, never mind anyone else's. But Rafferty had learned in the course of his career that appearances could be deceptive. Harris and the rest had been Barstaple's prey; he had stalked them as a fox stalks a rabbit. But back the weakest prey against a wall and they'll turn on you. Hadn't Crippen been meek, mild, cowed, just like Harris? For Crippen, love had been sufficient spur to find the courage for murder. Added to

80

his presumed anxiety about his continued employment, love could have been the spur in Harris's case, too. As Llewellyn had pointed out, it was possible Barstaple's murderer had been too blinded by hatred and misery to think as far as the possible consequences of ridding themselves of their immediate persecutor.

Rafferty questioned him further. 'You say you didn't go out to lunch as you had intended?'

Harris flushed. 'No. I – that is, as Ms Glossop told you, I had arranged to meet my wife just after midday. As that had fallen through, I didn't bother.'

Rafferty, who was always ready for his lunch, found this admission curious and his frank stare prompted Harris to provide a further explanation.

'My appetite had gone,' he said. 'I suffer from stomach ulcers. If I don't eat at set times they begin to play up and I don't feel much like eating at all. I forced a glass of milk down.'

Rafferty nodded. But he couldn't help wondering whether, in addition to the delay in eating and the upset over missing his lunch date, the conversation with Barstaple had ruined his appetite. He wondered what Harris and Barstaple had discussed. But that discovery could come later. For the moment, he wanted to set the scene, get the current crop of suspects fixed in his mind as individuals and find out who was where at what time. He turned back to Linda Luscombe.

'You said you shared Mr Barstaple's lunch. Was this a regular thing?'

'No.' She pulled a face. 'He normally went out for lunch. I learned yesterday that he was on a diet.'

'You weren't aware of this before yesterday?'

'No. I go to college and yesterday was my first day back.'

'So, what did you eat?'

'Just the prawns. Clive had some yoghurts in the fridge and he had a pot later, but I don't like yoghurt. At least, I presume he ate the yoghurt. He was about to open it when he had a telephone call – a long involved call and I came out of his office and left him to it. I suppose he ate the yoghurt later.'

Unlucky for his killer, Rafferty reflected as he recalled Sam Dally's comment. Or was it? Barstaple was still dead. Could it really matter to the killer that the delay had made pinpointing the source of the poison that much easier?

Maybe Llewellyn was right and he was crediting the killer with more intelligence and cunning than they actually possessed. It was possible, he supposed, though that didn't explain the removal of the poisoned yoghurt and its substitution; that smacked of a certain intelligence, a sly determination to muddy the waters.

Rafferty glanced round at the sea of faces. It was time to glean a few facts. 'Can any of you remember when Mr Barstaple placed the yoghurts in the fridge?'

They looked at one another and, as if by mutual decision, they all shook their heads. All but one. Amy Glossop seemed to have rallied. Certainly, she had no difficulty with her memory.

With a half-defiant look at the rest, she told him, 'He brought them in last Friday morning. Six of them, all different flavours. He'd done the same for the last few weeks since he started his diet. It had become quite a routine for him.'

'That's helpful,' Rafferty told her. 'Thank you.'

At this, Amy Glossop glanced at her colleagues, her expression smug, taunting even, the thought 'I've got nothing to hide' clearly etched.

They all ignored her, as if determined not to give her the

satisfaction of knowing she had just provided information that could be dangerous for one of them.

He turned back to Linda Luscombe. This was the first hint they'd had of any woman in Barstaple's life. He was curious to see how deep the relationship went. 'Had Mr Barstaple ever taken you out to lunch?'

'Sometimes.' The admission was reluctant. 'He could be quite insistent.'

'She means he was into sexual harassment as well as all the other kinds.'

This comment was drawn from Marian Steadman, whom Gallagher had introduced as the office first-aider, with the smiling comment that she doled out sympathy along with the Band Aids.

Marian Steadman was thirty-three. Rafferty was surprised the information from her staff record should immediately pop into his head. Attractive in an understated way, her open features were as different as possible from those of Amy Glossop. Even though she seemed to have no patience for evasion of any kind, she also had something of a maternal quality about her, as though she made a habit of taking on other people's troubles as her own. She reminded him of his ma, as did the forthright suggestion which followed.

'Why don't you tell him, Linda?' she encouraged. 'Let him know just what sort of man Clive Barstaple was.'

Linda shook her head. All at once she looked very young, very vulnerable.

Marian Steadman was evidently made of sterner stuff. Her voice brisk, she told Rafferty, 'Linda is a single mother. Her own mother, who used to look after her little girl during the daytime, recently remarried and moved away, so she's had to somehow find the money for child-minders. Clive Barstaple knew this and used it to pressurize her into being nice to him in exchange for promising her a job. That's the sort of man he was.'

More in sorrow than anger, she added, 'When I started here, Aimhurst and Son was a good firm to work for, a real family firm. Old Mr Aimhurst was a lovely man, a man of principle, firm morals, but caring, too. He'd never have taken on someone like Clive. God knows I didn't wish him dead, but it's not really surprising that it's come to this. Not really surprising that everyone here hated him.'

This brought a murmur of denial from her colleagues and she turned and quietly asked them, 'Do you really think there's any point in trying to pretend otherwise?' She shot an oblique glance in the direction of Amy Glossop and added, 'The Inspector will find out the situation here soon enough.'

Rafferty smiled and told her, 'I appreciate your honesty.' He paused. He liked to verify so-called facts from as many sources as possible, so now he went on, 'And this change has come about since the takeover and Mr Barstaple's appointment?'

Marian Steadman nodded. 'I suppose we all knew our jobs were in danger and that there would probably be a certain amount of weeding out in spite of young Mr Aimhurst's assurances to the contrary.'

As Rafferty noted the careful downplaying of the rationalization, she went on, 'But it was the way Clive went about his brief that was so – distasteful.' She frowned then as though searching for the best way to make him understand. 'He went out of his way to undermine an individual's confidence; whatever one did, he'd manage to find fault; pick, pick, pick. And then he made everyone terrified of falling sick. Take Bob Harris, for instance.'

Rafferty was beginning to wonder if Harris was the

office fall-guy. He glanced at the tight, pain-pinched features of Harris as Marian Steadman went on. 'He had an in-patient's appointment for an operation last month – one he's been waiting on for over a year. But he had to cancel. He didn't dare take the time to get his ulcers sorted out because he knew it would give Clive the excuse he wanted to get rid of him. The man was an out-and-out tyrant.'

Seven

After Marian Steadman's frank revelations, her colleagues, as though anxious to be thought equally as frank, were quick to back her up in her opinion of Barstaple's character. Even Amy Glossop, whom Rafferty suspected was the office spy given the speed with which the rest of the staff had isolated her, agreed that Barstaple could be 'a little difficult'.

Rafferty and Llewellyn made a start on taking the individual statements. It quickly became clear that, apart from Linda Luscombe, the rest of the staff had all had ample opportunity to plan and carry out Clive Barstaple's murder. Linda Luscombe, having only returned to work on the morning of the murder, had had a much more limited opportunity. Even this was reduced to zero when her colleagues backed up her statement that she hadn't entered the kitchen at all that day, it not being her turn on the rota to make the tea or coffee.

Fortunately, she wasn't the only suspect out of the running. Although Barstaple had chaired a sales meeting in the downstairs conference room with the firm's sales representatives and had also, in the previous week, instigated the last in a long line of appraisal interviews with these same reps, none of them had ventured into the main office or the kitchen, it being part of Barstaple's policy not to encourage the usual reps' idle chat.

Unfortunately, when it came to visits by other employees in the group, the statements were contradictory as to who had visited on what day and whether it had been the previous Thursday or the previous Friday; even Albert Smith, the apparently not over-security-conscious security guard, was uncertain as to details. Certainly none of their names appeared in the official visitors' book.

Rafferty sat back after he'd let Smith go, studied his steepled fingers and observed gruffly, 'This place seems to have been a veritable Piccadilly Circus in the last week. Isn't it just our luck?'

'At least we've got their names,' Llewellyn reminded him.

'Most of them,' Rafferty contradicted. 'There was one visitor whose identity nobody seems too sure about, apart from the probability that he's something to do with finance at Watts and Cutley's main office.' He scowled. 'I could wring Smith's neck. If the bloody man had done his job properly ours would be so much simpler.' He pushed himself to his feet. 'Come on. I asked Hal Gallagher to wait till last. He should be in the staff room. We'll interview him there.'

'Sorry to have kept you, Mr Gallagher,' Rafferty apologized as he and Llewellyn entered the otherwise empty staff room.

Gallagher shrugged. 'No matter. I've nothing to go home for. My wife died recently,' he explained, 'and to sit there alone only rubs my nose in how much I miss her. The apartment's just somewhere to eat and sleep now.' He smiled grimly at Rafferty. 'Funnily enough, if you can believe it after what you've learned this morning, I'd rather be here.'

Rafferty nodded. He'd been the same after his wife

Angie had died, though not for the same reasons. Guilt had driven him out of the home they had shared, where memories of her and the echo of their acrimonious rows were on every surface and on every stick of furniture; the dent in the door where she'd hurled a heavy ashtray at him; the stain in the carpet where a bottle of red wine had been sent flying; the remaining, mismatched crockery resulting from the nights she'd dumped his dinner, plate and all, in the bin when he'd had to work late. It had been a relief to move into his flat and away from all the accusatory contents of their old home.

The knowledge that he'd never really loved her had made him feel even more guilty and had hovered over him throughout the drawn-out period of her dying. Towards the end, gaunt from the ravages of the spreading cancer, she had taunted him with it; the pain had given her tongue a dreadfully bitter edge.

With difficulty, Rafferty pushed the distant past out of the forefront of his mind. Concentrating instead on the recent past, he said to Gallagher, 'I've asked everyone else this, sir, so, if you could let me know if you were here all day yesterday and if you've had any time off in the last week or so.'

'Sure. I was here all day yesterday. And no, I haven't had any time off recently.' Gallagher grinned. 'Hey, you heard what Marian Steadman said. I didn't dare. None of us did. You could say that Clive had made clear in that sly way of his that taking our full holiday entitlement wouldn't earn us the required brownie points in his report.'

Rafferty nodded. 'Perhaps you could tell me if anyone was alone in Mr Barstaple's office any time after lunch yesterday.'

He hoped to pin down the identity of anyone who had

had the opportunity to remove the poisoned yoghurt pot from the bin. The timing for this aspect of the murder was only a matter of hours instead of days and it might give them their lead. But in an attempt to avoid alerting the culprit of his interest in what could be a vital point, he had decided to limit the question to Gallagher. He now discovered his choice of confidant had been unfortunate.

Gallagher stared curiously at him. 'In his office? *After* lunch? But surely . . . ?' Gallagher's voice petered out and his expression became watchful.

Rafferty chose not to satisfy the American's curiosity and merely repeated his question. 'Can you recall anyone in particular?'

Gallagher shook his head firmly. 'Can't say I do.' He grinned again and his next words revealed that if it meant pointing the finger at Barstaple's murderer he wasn't likely to try too hard to remember. 'Always had a kinda shaky memory, me.' He glanced appraisingly at Rafferty. 'Weren't the rest of the staff able to help?'

Rafferty, unwilling to give Gallagher the idea that it was important, shrugged. 'I neglected to ask them. Never mind. It's only a minor point.'

Gallagher smiled. 'I wouldn't be sure the rest of the staff will remember either. Clive always kept them too busy for standing and staring. That was more his role.'

Although he thought the American was being deliberately obstructive, Rafferty couldn't help liking him. He suspected, in similar circumstances, he would behave the same. However, he was here in his policeman capacity not as a Dutch uncle and he opened his mouth to ask another question when Llewellyn saved him the trouble.

'What about Ms Glossop?' he asked Gallagher. 'She seems an observant kind of woman.'

Gallagher's smile faded. 'Well now, Sergeant, I reckon

you could be right there. Amy Glossop always did have a damn fine noticing way with her.'

Although he hadn't actually added the words, 'too bad', his whole manner implied that he wouldn't be exactly grief-stricken if Barstaple's murderer wasn't caught and punished. Given the character of the victim, Rafferty could sympathize with this attitude. It was clear Gallagher wasn't about to volunteer anything beyond the minimum.

It meant Rafferty had no choice but to select another confidant at the earliest opportunity. Llewellyn hadn't the only mind into which Amy Glossop's name sprang and he realized he should probably have put the question to her instead. She seemed the only one to have any reason for grief over Barstaple's death. And if she had been Barstaple's spy, she would presumably regret that his sudden death had also brought the loss of her little bit of power.

He brought the conversation to an end and thanked Gallagher for waiting. When the American had left, Rafferty didn't hurry away to continue the investigation elsewhere. Instead, he studied the noticeboard in the staff room, upon which, apart from the official notices, there was a display of photographs.

They had been taken at Christmas, that much was obvious, and were evidently at a staff function. Rafferty hardly recognized the happy, smiling faces; they were a far cry from the strained expressions he had encountered earlier; the strain not simply the result of being part of a murder investigation, but clearly pre-dating it by several months. He turned as he sensed someone hovering in the doorway It was Marian Steadman. Beyond her, in reception, he could see Bob Harris and Linda Luscombe chatting to Smith the security man. They were clearly waiting for Mrs Steadman. By now, it was lunchtime and from the snatches of their conversation that he caught it was apparent they had decided to go off to the pub and discuss the murder. Amy Glossop wasn't with them.

Rafferty had already put her down as the office spy, Barstaple's creature. And while, before his murder, it might have paid them to keep in with her, now there was no pretence that she was anything other than a pariah. As he looked through the window of reception he could see her leaving. A lonely figure, she was walking very slowly up the drive, her shoulders hunched.

Rafferty might have felt sorry for her had he not suspected that the forlorn air owed more to consciousness that her reign as boss's pet was at an end than to regret over her behaviour. He also felt it likely that her current 'untouchable' status would encourage her to seek ways of hitting back. And while he felt a certain distaste for tapping into such a source of information, he was too much the policeman to turn his back on it.

'How times change, Inspector.' Marian Steadman nodded at the noticeboard. 'Those photos were taken the Christmas before last. Mr Aimhurst senior was already in failing health. I suppose we'd realized it was the end of an era as, by then, most of us suspected he hadn't long left. It turned into something of a wake. We were determined to have a jolly time. Put like that, it sounds callous, but old Mr Aimhurst would have been the first to raise his glass. He was always such a lively man.'

She came and stood beside him and pointed to a particular picture. Central to the group was the jovial elderly man, white of hair and red of face, who made Rafferty think of Father Christmas.

'That's old Mr Aimhurst. A lovely old gentleman.' She sighed. 'It was a sad day for us when he died.'

Rafferty nodded and studied the photographs again.

'You certainly look as if you were having a good time.'
he smiled. 'Albert Smith, the security guard, particularly.
I hardly recognized him.'

In the photo that Rafferty was examining, Albert Smith
was sprawled across the lap of Marian Steadman, his thinning dark hair against her thicker tresses, while through
the thick lenses of his glasses his dark eyes glistened with
tears as he laughed uproariously at the camera.

Marian Steadman smiled. 'Disreputable lot we looked
there, didn't we? We weren't even drunk. Well, perhaps
Bertie was a little bit. He's always liked a drink. That's
probably why he forgot how long the self-timer on his
camera took to work.'

'Bertie?'

Quickly, she corrected herself. 'Albert, I mean. Albert
Smith. He took these pictures.' She gestured at the dozen
or so more professional-looking snaps pinned to the board.
'He's a keen amateur photographer. Only that one was
taken near the end of the evening and he wasn't thinking
quite as straight as he had been at the beginning, which
is why he had to rush to get into the picture. That's why
we're all laughing.'

Behind them, Llewellyn spoke up. 'But he's not employed
by Aimhurst's. He's employed by Guardian Security. I'm
surprised he should be invited to a staff function.'

'I told you, we were one big happy family. Of course
Albert was invited. Everyone who worked here, in whatever
capacity, always went. That was our last staff party. Watts
and Cutley have made it clear they don't run to such things.'

'Still,' Llewellyn commented, 'I imagine many firms
have to limit expenditure on such items.'

Marian Steadman laughed. 'Not this one. You could
say the Aimhurst Widget puts it in the position of the
privatized utility companies with a captive market and

little in the way of competition. Aimhurst's has always been a profitable business. Why else do you think Watts and Cutley were interested?'

Her words confirmed what Hal Gallagher had already told them.

'But old Mr Aimhurst believed in sharing at least some of the profits with those who produced them and Watts and Cutley don't, as I'm sure you've discovered by now. That's why there'll be no Christmas treats for the staff, why poor Bob Harris spends his time tipping medicine down his throat, why we're all terrified of losing our jobs and why morale's at rock bottom.

'Even Amy Glossop has her own reasons for being frightened about the future. Her mother's in a private nursing home,' she explained, 'and it costs the earth to keep her there. I've met her.' The bleak expression in her warm brown eyes made it clear this had not been a pleasant experience. Her next words confirmed it. 'Amy Glossop's mother is not a very nice woman. She led Amy a dog's life before their GP persuaded her to move into the home. Of course, Springvale Lodge is very expensive and even though I know Amy has a small private income, if she lost her job here she'd have no choice but to have her mother return home to live with her. Not a prospect to be relished, I assure you. Knowing that, I can understand why Amy behaved as she did. Lacking either beauty or brains I'd guess she concluded that currying favour with Clive Barstaple was the only option open to her.'

She sighed. 'And much good it'll do her now. Though I doubt that Clive Barstaple would have recommended keeping her on in any case. Not once she'd served her purpose. She would have been regarded as expendable, like most of the rest of us. She must have known that.'

93

When she had gone and made for the pub with her colleagues, Rafferty glanced at Llewellyn and commented,
'No shortage of suspects, anyway, Daff. They certainly
sound a desperate enough bunch.'

Llewellyn nodded. 'And desperate men and women do
desperate things.'

'Including murder.' Rafferty paused and thoughts of
Superintendent Bradley prompted him to add, 'Maybe
the murder of Clive Barstaple will give the less com-
passionate bosses in this country pause for thought –
of the "there but for the grace of God go I" variety.'
He hoped so, anyway. With a bit of luck, too, it
would give Superintendent Bradley an uneasy moment
or two wondering if one of the underlings had laced his
morning coffee with something richer than Jersey cream.
That was another option, Rafferty comforted himself.
Always supposing he hadn't come up with a solution
to the dodgy suit dilemma before the wedding.

Back at the station, they began checking through the
staff statements, comparing them to see if there were
any discrepancies they had missed.

As they had already discovered, of the staff past and
present, Linda Luscombe was the only one definitely out
of the running. One down, nine hundred and ninety-nine
to go, mused Rafferty, as he thought of all the possible
victims of Barstaple's past rationalizations, any one of
whom, in the interim, might have got a job with Watts
and Cutley or one of their subsidiaries.

But, for the moment, he concentrated on the staff
at Aimhurst's. And the last of the staff to leave the
office yesterday evening had been Hal Gallagher and
Marian Steadman, so either of them would have had
the opportunity to switch the yoghurt cartons and remove

94

Barstaple's lap-top, which, Amy Glossop had revealed, Barstaple had been using in his office on the day of his murder. So, too, would Albert Smith, the security guard. He had been alone in the premises from about five thirty, when Gallagher and Marian Steadman had left, till the cleaners had arrived an hour later. Though, like the cleaners, Smith worked for another firm, so unless they discovered a past connection with Barstaple he would have no reason to wish him dead. But, as Llewellyn now pointed out, even if there was no past connection Smith wasn't entirely out of the running.

'He said he didn't see or hear Barstaple after the office staff left. Doesn't that strike you as odd?'

Rafferty stared at him. Slowly he nodded.

'Barstaple would have been feeling dreadfully ill. Even if he felt unable to leave the washroom to seek help, he could have still opened the door and shouted. The toilets are at the top of the stairs and the reception desk is only a few yards around the corner from the bottom of the stairs, so Smith must surely have heard him.'

'True.' Rafferty's lips tightened. 'Perhaps, as soon as forensic have finished and the staff are back at work, we should organize a little test. See if Albert's hearing is up to par.'

Llewellyn nodded. 'Albert Smith is also the first to arrive in the morning, so would have the opportunity to both poison the yoghurt and substitute the empty strawberry carton with the hazelnut flavour one in the wastebin, with no likelihood of anyone seeing him. And that, assuming the killer didn't supply their own pot of poisoned yoghurt as Dr Dally suggested, doesn't apply in regard to the other suspects.'

'True again. But,' Rafferty added, 'where's the motive? Unless he was one of Barstaple's earlier rationalization

victims I can't see why Smith would want to murder
Barstaple. Like the cleaners, he's employed by outsiders.
There again, I suppose Barstaple was capable of being as
nasty to other people's staff as he was to his own. His
cruel "moron" jibe at Eric Penn proves that.'

They worked their way steadily through the rest of the
statements. As nothing else odd revealed itself, Rafferty
transferred his attentions to the visitors' book that Hal
Gallagher had supplied.

There had been twenty outside callers to Aimhurst's
offices since Friday morning when, according to Amy
Glossop, Barstaple had brought a pack of six yoghurts
into the office. So he had presumably either purchased
them earlier that morning or on the previous evening.

Rafferty had got the station to contact the local office
of the dairy that delivered to Aimhurst's offices. They
had supplied the home telephone number of the milkman
concerned, who had denied that Barstaple had purchased
the yoghurt from him. If true, it confirmed what Albert
Smith had already told them; that Jim, the milkman, never
went into the offices and had certainly not done so in the
last week or two.

And as Clive Barstaple started work a good hour and a
half after the milkman made his delivery to the office, he
would have been unable to give him an additional order
verbally. On questioning the fact that the firm had a milk
delivery when they already had a drinks machine, he
had learned that Barstaple refused to drink the machine
coffee. Surprisingly, he didn't expect the staff to, either.
As long as the staff paid for the extra milk, he had made
no objections to the order being increased. The usual milk
order was the province of Hal Gallagher, who had charge
of petty expenditure.

So, Barstaple had either ordered the yoghurts from his

own milkman, if he had one – something which Lilley was supposed to be checking – or he had bought them with the rest of his groceries. He had despatched Lilley early to Barstaple's home, firstly, to have another hunt for the rationalization report that Barstaple had been working on and, secondly, after Sam Dally had completed the post-mortem and reported back, to hunt for any yoghurt receipt and catch the milkman on his rounds.

Rafferty checked his watch. It was now nearly 1.30 p.m. Hopefully, Lilley would ring in soon and let him know if he'd found out anything.

As if on cue, his phone rang. It was Lilley.

'I've found out where Barstaple bought the yoghurt, guv,' he said. 'He bought it off his own milkman on Friday morning.'

'And did he speak to the milkman or just leave a note?' Rafferty, by now convinced that Barstaple was the kind of man to make enemies wherever he went, prayed Lilley would confirm it had been the former. He didn't relish the investigation spreading over to the neighbours; if the milkman had left the yoghurt on Barstaple's doorstep, anyone would have had an opportunity to tamper with it.

'He not only spoke to the milkman, he took the milk and yoghurt straight from his hands,' Lilley confirmed to Rafferty's relief. 'It was his usual day for paying the bill, you see.'

'I've found out something else as well, guv.' Lilley paused. 'The victim seems to have gone in for some odd sexual practices.'

Rafferty frowned. 'What do you mean?'

Lilley explained. 'I've found bondage gear at his home as well as articles of ladies' underwear.'

'Maybe the underwear was left by old girlfriends,' Rafferty commented.

'I've also found some capsules of amyl nitrate.'

As Rafferty knew, amyl nitrate was used, along with controlled suffocation techniques, to heighten sexual pleasure. It was anybody's guess whether Barstaple had gone in for his perversions alone or had had company, though, from reading the several cases in the press in recent years, Rafferty recalled that the lonely men who got their sexual kicks from dicing with death usually did it alone.

It was a side to Clive Barstaple that Rafferty hadn't expected; the flash Porsche had inclined him to the automatic assumption that the dead man would have had a selection of flashy lady friends to go with it. His sexual harassment of Linda Luscombe had also inclined him to the view. But from what Lilley had found out that now seemed less likely.

He sighed. Wasn't it enough, he thought, that the wretched man had been a sadist at work without being a masochist at home as well? 'What about that rationalization report he was supposed to be working on?' Rafferty asked. 'Still no sign of it?'

'No.'

'Keep looking. And question the neighbours again. Hopefully one of them might know a bit more about Barstaple's love life than you've so far learned. I want to know about any lady friends, particularly any he'd recently upset. He seemed to have a gift for upsetting people.'

'He didn't have any girlfriends, guv,' Lilley insisted. 'For the record, he doesn't appear to have had any men friends, either. His cleaning lady, a Mrs Waterman, arrived ten minutes ago. According to her, and she's worked for him since he moved here from north London three months ago, the victim never entertained. Or if he did, he certainly never left the evidence piled in the kitchen for her to clean up. There was only ever the one set of everything waiting for her when she arrived.'

'Speak to the neighbours again, anyway. Maybe it's just that he didn't believe in feeding any girl- or boyfriends.'

Lilley said he'd check again and Rafferty rang off.

Llewellyn had been called away whilst Rafferty was on the phone. Now he returned, carrying a number of sheets of paper, which he told Rafferty contained the names and addresses of the staff Barstaple had caused to be rationalized in the past.

With dismay, Rafferty noted that Llewellyn's paper collection looked formidable. Barstaple had evidently practised his rationalization skills for some very large businesses. And given that Albert Smith seemed to have waved everyone but complete strangers through with an utter lack of either formality or security, they'd all have to be checked out. It was possible that any one of them had a connection with Aimhurst's or Watts and Cutley. He told Llewellyn what Lilley had discovered at the victim's home.

'Bondage gear, you say?' Llewellyn shook his head. 'He must have been a very lonely and unhappy man.'

'Why do you say that?' Rafferty demanded. His sympathies were with the workers; bosses had never been his favourite people. Besides, as he told Llewellyn, if Barstaple had been so lonely and unhappy the remedy had been in his own hands, unlike his staff. A man who went out of his way to make others' lives miserable must expect to be friendless.

A faint sigh escaped Llewellyn. 'That's a rather simplistic view, if I may say so.'

'You have said so, and no ifs about it,' Rafferty observed. 'I suppose you're going to tell me he probably had a grim, emotionally deprived childhood with a mother who didn't love him and a father who beat him. I've no sympathy with such excuses for behaving like a bastard.' Rafferty, whose opinions, moods, and sympathies were apt to change with the weather, conveniently forgot that during the course of their last case together his own sympathies had swayed with every passing breeze.

'All I'm saying is that no one is all bad. If you dig deep enough you'll find a reason for his behaviour, which would at least explain if not excuse it.'

'Remind me to tell Sam to have another hunt around Barstaple's insides to see if he can't dig this reason up. Though I doubt he'll find anything more than he has already. The only reason he ground the staff into the dust was because he enjoyed it. No,' Rafferty corrected himself, 'that's probably not the only reason. You heard Hal Gallagher – I bet if Barstaple managed to push the staff into either leaving or providing him with grounds for legitimate dismissal before the six-month deadline, he was in for a nice fat bonus.'

He slammed the visitors' book shut. 'Those are the reasons for his behaviour, Dafyd: natural-born nastiness and greed. God, man, there are enough accounts in the papers of bosses of profitable concerns sacking workers or cutting their pay or perks while the bosses award themselves ever larger salary increases. Double standards and hypocrisy. No wonder the country's going to the dogs.'

As Llewellyn had the sense to keep quiet and not stoke him further, Rafferty finally ran out of steam. 'Anyway,' he added gruffly, 'at least now we know when and where he bought the yoghurt. It's an advance. Can you get Birmingham nick to question Aimhurst's other cleaner? What's her name? Mrs Flowers. Might as well find out what, if anything, she can tell us.'

Llewellyn nodded.

Rafferty glanced again at Llewellyn's bundle of paper-work. 'And before we set to work checking the names on that great long list or in this,' he slapped the visitors' book, 'I suggest we speak to the boss of Allways Cleaning Services to get the backgrounds on the cleaners and see if we can't at least remove some more names from the suspect list.

'But, before we do that, I think it might pay us to have another chat with Amy Glossop. As Gallagher said, she's a noticing sort of woman. Maybe she noticed more than she's so far told us. I imagine we'll find her at home.'

Eight

Amy Glossop lived in one of five flats above the little parade of shops off Elmhurst High Street. Her flat, like the others in the row, had its entrance round the back of the shops, up a private alleyway. The alleyway was unlaid, it was still raining, and they squelched their way along to Amy Glossop's door which, inevitably, was the last in the row.

Her entrance was unexpectedly private, as a six-foot brick wall separated her garden from her neighbour and another on the other side separated her from the side street.

Unlike the rest of the row, Amy Glossop's garden was well-cared for. Even though it was February, the mean little strip was far from bare and several glossy, easy-care evergreens broke up the otherwise empty borders.

Rafferty noticed there was a large bare patch in one corner which didn't match the other three, each of which contained a sizeable evergreen. The planting was so symmetrical that the naked corner drew the eye and filled his mind with suspicion. Had Amy Glossop torn out a rhododendron bush and destroyed it before the police had a chance to notice it? He confided his thoughts to Llewellyn.

The Welshman, busy scraping the mud off the high gloss of his Italian leather shoes, merely commented that if a rhododendron bush had been planted there and she had removed it to conceal her guilt, it would be a simple matter to plant something in its place.

'In February?'

'It wouldn't matter if the replacement plant died,' Llewellyn pointed out. 'To hide the gap, she could continue to replace it with something else till spring arrived. The fact that she hasn't indicates that she has nothing to hide.'

'Or that that's what she wants us to think.'

'I thought she was your star witness, not your prime suspect.'

'I'm not so sure. I think Marian Steadman was right. Why would a man like Barstaple recommend that Amy Glossop be kept on the payroll when she had served her purpose? The answer is that he wouldn't. He strikes me as the type to use people and discard them once he's sucked all the juice out of them. Amy Glossop must have suspected as much. After all, she's had the evidence of her own mother in front of her all her life. She seems cut from a similar mould to Barstaple.'

Trying to avoid the drips, they huddled under the narrow lintel over Amy Glossop's door as they waited for her to answer their knock. It occurred to Rafferty that he was about to do his damnedest to suck the remaining juice from the woman.

As he had anticipated, Amy Glossop was at home. And, as they followed her up the stairs from her front door to her flat, Rafferty found himself thinking further about what Marian Steadman had said concerning Amy Glossop's mother. Settled in a worn armchair in the living room, he experienced the feeling of pity that had eluded him earlier. It was obvious that money was tight; everything in the room was faded, shabby, crying out for replacement.

There were cleaner, bare areas on the walls where pictures had been and the furniture had a rearranged air indicating that everything that could be sold had been sold. He could imagine every spare pound, every spare penny would be squirreled away so she could continue to keep her mother at Springvale Lodge.

'Not a very nice woman' was how Marian Steadman had described Amy Glossop's mother. He guessed it was a description she would not bestow lightly. And as he studied a photograph of someone he assumed could only be Amy's mother, he felt she was right. If character showed up in the face, 'not very nice' hardly covered it.

Simply put, the woman looked a monster. She must weigh at least twenty stone and, in shape and colour, her face resembled nothing so much as a pasty suet pudding. From somewhere above the middle of this heavy slab of a face two cold eyes gazed with animal slyness rather than true intelligence. She must have had her hair styled especially for the photo, he noted, because, incongruously, her light brown hair was a mass of candyfloss curls.

Rafferty shuddered. Under the shapeless brown dress he could trace the outline of her thighs and each looked as thick as his waist. He wondered why Amy Glossop had the photo on such prominent display. Perhaps, he thought, it was used as a reminder of what would return if she could no longer keep up the payments for the home that caged the monster mother.

Now he understood why Amy Glossop had behaved as she had. He'd have sold his soul to keep such a mother at arms' length.

Under Llewellyn's introductory chat, Rafferty became aware that Amy Glossop's sharp, bird-bright eyes were studying him. The realization brought him up short. He might feel sorry for her but that didn't mean he had to lower his guard. Quickly he interrupted Llewellyn and brought the conversation round to Barstaple's murder and how he thought she could help them.

Unlike Hal Gallagher, Amy Glossop was obviously willing to spill any number of beans, though, like Gallagher, she seemed to find his question puzzling and didn't trouble to hide the fact.

'But why should it matter who was in his office? The kitchen was where he kept the food for his lunch. When you questioned me before you hardly seemed interested in that. Surely you should be more interested in who was in the kitchen and had occasion to tamper with the food than—'

Rafferty decided to be frank with her. He guessed it was likely to be the most rewarding route. She was the kind of woman who liked to be in the know. It would encourage her – if she needed encouragement – to share whatever information she had.

'Knowing who had been in the kitchen before lunch on the day of Mr Barstaple's death wouldn't be much help, Ms Glossop. The poison that killed him was in the yoghurt, not the prawns, and that could have been tampered with at any time since Mr Barstaple put it in the fridge last Friday.' He didn't bother mentioning Sam Dally's suggestion that someone could also have bought the same make of yoghurt and added the poison at home.

She stared at him with narrowed eyes and then slowly nodded. 'Of course.' With her head tilted to one side just like the bird to which Rafferty had likened her, she added, 'Now I understand why you want to know who was in his office that afternoon. There were two pots of yoghurt, weren't there?'

She didn't wait for Rafferty to answer but went on

eagerly, 'That's why you want to know who was alone in his office yesterday afternoon. I can't imagine why I didn't realize before. As I told you, Mr Barstaple brought half a dozen yoghurts into the office on Friday. Since he started his diet he always ate one a day. He was very regular in his habits, which meant there should still be two yoghurts left. But there aren't, are there? There's only one.'

Llewellyn broke in and quickly asked, 'How do you know that?'

'It's perfectly simple,' she answered. 'I always make – made – Mr Barstaple's tea and coffee, so I know there were three pots of yoghurt in the fridge yesterday morning and two in the afternoon, hazelnut and raspberry. Yet I overheard that young policeman, Smales I think his name is, say something about a hazelnut yoghurt being the only carton in his bin. It struck me as odd and I've been thinking about it ever since.' She sat back, and, with a brief animation, added, 'It's obvious somebody switched the pots.' She frowned. 'But why would they? I don't understand.'

Rafferty, impressed by her natural powers of observation and deduction, waited to see if she would find even more clinching answers to explain the switch than Dally had managed. But not being privy to Dally's other confidences placed her at a disadvantage in this respect. She was unable to either answer the question herself or encourage Rafferty to divulge his thoughts on the subject. He was surprised she didn't press him about it.

She had yet to answer his original question he realized and now he asked again, 'Can you remember who was alone in Mr Barstaple's office on Wednesday afternoon? If you noticed, that is.'

This was a direct challenge to her observational skills,

106

something she evidently took great pride in, and she told him sharply, 'Of course I noticed. All of my colleagues were in Mr Barstaple's office alone at some time yesterday afternoon. Mr Gallagher, Bob Harris, and Marian Steadman; in that order.'

'And do you remember the times?'

She nodded. 'They were all in there after three o'clock. I remember because that's when I made Mr Barstaple's coffee. He drank it, closed up his lap-top and went downstairs for his monthly meeting with the sales team.'

'So it was when you made Mr Barstaple's coffee that you noticed there were definitely still two yoghurts in the fridge?'

She nodded.

'Did you notice if any of those three members of staff were in the kitchen after you'd made Mr Barstaple's coffee?' They'd have had to be, Rafferty realized, if one of them was the murderer and if the hazelnut yoghurt pot was to be emptied and put in Barstaple's bin.

'No,' Amy Glossop admitted. 'But that's not to say they weren't. I left the main office several times that afternoon to go to the cloakroom or to use the photocopier which is in a little cubbyhole at the far end of the office, so any one of them could easily have gone in there then and, apart from Mr Barstaple himself who was downstairs talking to Albert Smith when I left, Marian Steadman and Hal Gallagher were the last to leave that night. Which would have given them even more opportunity to switch the yoghurt pots.' She sat back with the air of having emptied her own pot. Her efforts seemed to have tired her.

Rafferty didn't bother to point out that she had forgotten to mention that, by being able to supply such information, she must also have been one of the last to leave on

Wednesday evening. And, if she discovered that she had served her purpose and would soon be thrown on the scrapheap with the rest of her middle-aged colleagues, she would have a strong motive for murdering Barstaple herself. He glanced again at the picture of her mother and felt the same revulsion. Anything that would postpone the return of the monster would, he was sure, be grabbed with both hands. And, whatever else it did, Barstaple's death and the apparent disappearance of the report would certainly delay the carrying out of Watts and Cutley's rationalization plans.

Amy Glossop had one of those strangely fluid faces that made the concealment of her real emotions difficult. She seemed unaware of this, but Rafferty found he could trace the direction of her thoughts in the changing expressions; loneliness, anger, resentment. The last but one to cross her face was determination; a resolve to get revenge on the colleagues who had cold-shouldered her that morning, Rafferty guessed.

As though following the thought with the deed, she said, 'There is one thing I thought I ought to mention.' She paused and assumed a reluctant air. 'But I wouldn't want you to get the wrong idea. I'm sure it's not important at all and I wouldn't want to get poor Bob Harris into trouble—' She broke off. Rafferty adopted a look of polite enquiry and waited.

She simpered. 'But there, I suppose it's my duty to tell you. You know why he really lost his appetite on Wednesday, don't you?'

She didn't wait for Rafferty's response, but carried on quickly as if she had managed to convince herself that the disloyalty would somehow be lessened if she told them as speedily as possible. 'You already know that he'd arranged to meet his estranged wife just after midday

108

and this was the first time he'd managed to persuade her to meet him.'

Rafferty nodded and Llewellyn then asked the logical question. 'Surely such a meeting would have been better arranged in the evening? If it was so important to him, I would have thought he would wish to devote more time than he could take during the working day.'

'But that's just it, you see, he did. He tried to get his wife to agree to an evening meeting, but she insisted the meeting was held during lunchtime on a weekday. I got the impression it was a kind of test, as I gather that one of the reasons they separated was because Bob's weakness had, in the past, infuriated her. She felt he put work before her and had often let her down on social occasions because work demands kept him late in the office. She knew we're kept very busy because several staff have left and that we often have to skip lunch to get through the work. She probably wanted to see if he would put her first this time and defy Mr Barstaple if he asked him to skip lunch again.' She broke off and with a sigh probably owing more to spite than sorrow, added, 'I think she'd given him some kind of ultimatum.'

Rafferty nodded. His late wife had made similar difficulties. Poor Harris, he thought; with the demands of a wife on the one hand and Barstaple on the other, he had been in a no-win situation. 'Please go on.'

'Bob being Bob, had built up his hopes that this meeting would be the start of a full reconciliation. I doubt there's any chance of that now. As he told you, Mr Barstaple called him into his office just as he was leaving to meeting his wife and kept him back for half an hour.'

Rafferty hunched forward. 'Let me get this clear. Are you saying that Clive Barstaple knew about this meeting and deliberately wrecked it?' From what Rafferty had learned of the victim's character it was the sort of thing he might try.

Whether to conceal her real feelings about Barstaple or because she really felt she owed him her loyalty, when asked to do the dirty on him she immediately went into denial. 'Oh, no, I'm sure Mr Barstaple wouldn't have done such a thing. Admittedly, the state of Bob's marriage was common knowledge in the office and so was the lunch date he'd arranged and his hopes for a reconciliation, but I really don't believe that Mr Barstaple would deliberately prevent him going.'

As though she recognized that this last took some swallowing, she gave up trying to defend the indefensible and instead went on the attack. 'But it doesn't really matter, does it, whether Mr Barstaple knew of this meeting or not? Surely, the question is whether Bob Harris thought Mr Barstaple had deliberately ruined his hopes?'

She had a point, Rafferty conceded, though it seemed unlikely that Harris had brought poison into the office on the, admittedly, fifty-fifty chance that Barstaple would do just that. And although he couldn't say that he hadn't, Amy Glossop's spiteful tittle-tattle made him point it out. 'He would hardly have come to the office that day prepared to poison Mr Barstaple. He can't have been sure he'd have reason to do so.'

Artlessly, she told him, 'But he had other reasons. Lots of them; weeks of worry as to whether he would keep his job, the accompanying stress and strain. He was never the most competent man and I'm afraid Mr Barstaple found poor Bob's indifferent performance something of a trial. He often complained to me about it. And then I know Bob's ulcers give him a great deal of pain.'

Perhaps she felt she had burned her bridges and might as well tell all. For whatever reason, her earlier show of reluctance had certainly vanished and now she proceeded to strengthen the case against Harris. 'I once read of a case where a man took to carrying poison around with him as some kind of talisman, as a morale-boosting reminder that he could rid himself of his tormentor at any time, without ever intending to actually use it. Then his boss did something that this man regarded as beyond the pale and he killed him.'

Her words reminded Rafferty that Bob Harris had mentioned he'd got a glass of milk from the kitchen that day for his lunch, and that he'd got it immediately after his little chat with Barstaple. If he'd come prepared, the impulse to inject the poison through the plastic bottom of the yoghurt carton would take a matter of moments.

They already knew that Bob Harris had been alone in Barstaple's office that afternoon, which meant that he had had the opportunity to both administer the poison and swap the yoghurt containers in the bin. And it had been his name on the rota that afternoon for making the tea for the other staff. He had made it after Amy Glossop had made Clive Barstaple's, whose needs always took precedence.

Admittedly, according to Amy Glossop, whom he was beginning to dislike all over again, two more of the staff had had similar opportunities. But, so far, Harris was the only one Barstaple was known to have damaged that important six hours before he had died; the six hours the particular poison took to produce its deadly effect.

Of course it might mean nothing. They'd already concluded that the poison could have been put into the carton of yoghurt at any time. Still, for Harris, it was a damaging discovery. It was also interesting that Amy Glossop should try so hard to incriminate her colleagues. Was resentment of them her only motive? Or was there some other demon

111

driving her? She was the type to go in for eavesdropping. In order to have something to offer Barstaple so that he would give her preferential treatment, she would have had no choice but to poke and pry. Maybe all her poking and prying had revealed Barstaple's true intentions with regard to her future; that he intended to rationalize her, too. How would such a woman feel at the discovery? Rafferty wondered. Enraged and vengeful? Or fearful and despairing?

It was impossible to know. Maybe it would be a mixture of all four. He just wished they could find the damn rationalization report that Barstaple had been working on. Then they'd know for certain what Barstaple's intentions had been, not only for Amy Glossop but for the rest of the staff.

Llewellyn, polite as ever, said as they stood up to go, 'You've been very helpful, Ms Glossop. If there's anything else you remember . . .'

Rafferty was sure there was plenty, but he suspected she would dole out any information piece by piece so as to increase the period of her self-importance.

To his surprise, he found he had misjudged her. And as if she now regretted directing their suspicions to Bob Harris, who would make poor sport, she said, 'In spite of what I've said to you, I can't believe Bob Harris would have the gumption to kill. Besides, it wasn't Bob who had the furious row with Clive. That was Mr Gallagher. And he'd have the gumption for anything.'

Nine

Rafferty and Llewellyn glanced at one another then sat down again. Rafferty wondered how much more tittle-tattle Amy Glossop had stored in her mouse-brown head. He suddenly felt impelled to warn her that if she knew anything else that might be damaging to a possible murderer she ought to tell them now.

But she insisted there was nothing else. He wasn't sure he believed her.

'When was this argument?' he asked.

Amy Glossop paused as if considering. Rafferty guessed this was for show. She probably knew to the minute and had hugged the information to herself since she had known of Barstaple's murder. 'It was last Friday. After everybody else had gone home.' Her bright brown eyes narrowed. 'I suppose Mr Gallagher waited till then so there would be no witnesses. He didn't count on me coming back.'

Rafferty wondered what Gallagher had done to earn this stab in the back and thought he could guess. Amy Glossop was a soured, embittered woman. An attractive, outgoing male like Hal Gallagher would have found it hard to hide his contempt for her; that would be enough to earn her hatred.

Bob Harris wouldn't be much of a threat to her sexual dignity; he would, Rafferty thought again, be poor sport.

113

Not that that had stopped her supplying them with damaging information. But Hal Gallagher was a different matter. No doubt that was why she had saved her most damaging evidence till last.

Rafferty eased his buttocks off the sagging cushion, and asked, 'Do you know what this argument was about?'

She looked disappointed to have to admit that she didn't. 'I'd already left the office once, you see, but had forgotten my umbrella. And as I'm sure one of these cleaners stole the last one I'd left here, I came back for it. I heard them as I came up the stairs. Going at it hammer and tongs, they were. They were both shouting, though, of course, Mr Gallagher has such a huge bellow that his voice quite drowned out whatever Clive was saying. It was only as I reached the top of the stairs that Hal Gallagher paused for breath and I was able to make out what Clive said. It certainly shut Hal Gallagher up.'

Amy Glossop obviously had a heightened sense of drama because now she paused and looked expectantly at them. Obligingly Rafferty offered the required prompt. 'And what did he say?'

'I'll never forget it.' She looked as though she was preparing to break off again, but a glance at Rafferty's impatient expression had her hurrying on. 'Clive told Hal Gallagher he'd better be careful as he – Clive, that is – wasn't the only one with something to hide. And that if it came to it he had something on Hal Gallagher that was far more damaging than a few questionable deals, which anyway Mr Plumley already knew about. Perks, he called them.'

Amy Glossop pulled a face. 'That's all I caught. They must have heard me then as they both shut up. At least, Hal Gallagher slammed out of Clive's office right away. Though he was still at his own desk when I left.' She broke off again and gazed from one to the other eagerly as she suggested, 'Perhaps he'd already decided on more drastic measures. After all, Clive's dead. Whatever damaging knowledge he had on Hal Gallagher died with him – and less than a week after their row. Bit of a coincidence, don't you think?'

Amy Glossop had given them a lot to chew over. And as they left her flat and drove to the offices of Allways Cleaning Services, Rafferty remarked on the last thing she had told them.

'So, now we know that not only was the victim a thoroughly nasty piece of work and into strange sexual practices, but that he was also a bit of a crook.' He paused, then added mischievously, 'The poor unhappy bastard.'

Llewellyn, as expected, failed to rise to the bait. As he turned the car into Queen Street and past the front of the police station, Rafferty asked, 'So, what do you reckon Barstaple could have had on Gallagher?'

Llewellyn gave a tiny shrug. 'I've no idea. Maybe we'll never find out now as I shouldn't think Gallagher is about to tell us. He may even attempt to deny the argument ever happened, though I doubt that. He'd be more likely to invent something plausible to explain it as he must know Amy Glossop would tell us about it as soon as possible. He must have been surprised that she didn't do so this morning. The delay has given him time to come up with something good.'

Rafferty nodded. He suspected that Gallagher would have plenty of street-smarts. He'd certainly be smart enough to come up with a plausible reason for the argument; something that didn't provide him with a motive for murder.

115

Either way, they'd have to question him again. They'd have to question them all again. Certainly, vindictive or not, as far as it went, Amy Glossop's evidence had the ring of truth. It had narrowed the odds considerably and gave them a fighting chance of finding Barstaple the Bastard's killer. Wasn't that a stroke of luck? Rafferty wryly asked himself.

Ross Arnold, the boss of Allways Cleaning Services, the firm that supplied Aimhurst's cleaning staff, was a superficially friendly man of about thirty-five. Broad, with a too-easy smile, his apparently open manner appeared designed to disarm.

As soon as he entered Arnold's office and saw the set-up, Rafferty suspected that the task of clearing a few names off his suspects' list wasn't going to be quite as simple as he'd hoped – because Allways struck Rafferty as one of those fly-by-night concerns that were always one step ahead of the taxman. Its one-room office was situated above a dry cleaner's and housed a mobile phone, a scratched, secondhand desk and a card-index box. That was it. Its location, close to the railway station, was also indicative of the wide-boy nature of Arnold's operation. The location would ensure a quick flit should the Inland Revenue start showing an interest.

His suspicions were almost immediately confirmed. After asking for background details of those of his employees who worked at Aimhurst's, Arnold did his best to oblige, but it was obvious that the man's best would fall far short of requirements.

He opened his card-index file with a great show of willingness, but the sparsity of information it contained made it only too plain that his workers were of the more casual sort.

'Is this all you have, Mr Arnold?' Llewellyn asked quietly. 'Where are your payroll records, for instance?'

Arnold, of course, had his answer off pat. 'They're with my accountant. It's my year end, you see. I like to have everything nicely squared off.'

I just bet you do, thought Rafferty, who recognized a wide-boy when he saw one. 'Perhaps we can have the name of this accountant,' he suggested drily.

Rather to his surprise, Arnold supplied a name. Unsurprisingly, the name of Arnold's finance man was one of that breed of accountants at the less salubrious end of the adding and subtracting echelon. He was also one who had more addresses than the Queen. 'And where might we find Mr Cohen this week?'

'I believe he's away at the moment,' Arnold told them. 'Got a villa in Spain, I understand.'

With all the rest of the Costa Crooks presumably. 'How convenient. Going to work on your tax return during his hols, was he?'

Arnold shrugged.

Rafferty thought he was going to have to come the hard man. But Llewellyn, that man of stern principles and even sterner morals, saved him the trouble. Of course, the Welshman had the advantage of actually caring that the taxman was being defrauded.' That's simply not good enough, Mr Arnold,' Llewellyn told him. 'We're in the middle of a murder inquiry. We need information about the staff who worked at Aimhurst's and we need it now.'

Arnold protested. 'Most of my workers are casuals, drifters, students and the like. They come and they go.' He threw his hands in the air as if to seek their sympathy as he tried to justify himself. 'What can I do? I have to employ what I can get. It means I have little information on any of them; often just a name and a contact number.' He shrugged, as much as to imply that, left to himself, he would prefer to run a more stable business.

Rafferty doubted it. It seemed likely that anyone who wanted a job without too many questions being asked would find one here with few problems, with cash in hand and no paperwork. As he'd had a few jobs like that in his youth, Rafferty was in no position to put the moral boot in. Not so Llewellyn.

'And would some of these casuals be illegal immigrants, Mr Arnold? Desperate people who'll work for whatever pittance you choose to pay them? Some people would call you a parasite.'

'Now look here,' Arnold blustered. 'I don't—'

'No. You look,' Llewellyn told him sharply. 'Among your records or in your memory. I don't care which. We both know that the cleaning staff at Aimhurst's were among your more long-standing employees. You shouldn't find it too difficult to supply a few meagre details.'

Arnold blustered and wriggled a while longer, but Llewellyn was implacable. Rafferty admired Llewellyn's staunch principles. The trouble was he'd admire them a whole lot more if they weren't likely soon to be directed at him. Because Arnold wasn't the only one currently trying to wriggle his way out of a predicament. When Superintendent Bradley found out about his ma and her 'bargain' suit, he and Llewellyn would be labelled with far harder names than 'parasite'. Bent coppers, for instance.

Rafferty sighed and wondered why life always had to be so difficult. 'Perhaps, Mr Arnold, while you're thinking about the names of the staff that my colleague has requested, you'll answer another question.'

'If I can.' Arnold's ready smile was becoming frayed around the edges.

'This one shouldn't tax you too much,' he reassured. 'It was just a question of your receipts and their nature. I suppose we can take it that the firms you have contracts with all pay by cheque?' From the look on Arnold's face the answer to this was likely to land him in another predicament. Rafferty could almost feel sorry for the man.

Arnold eased the shirt collar from around his fat neck as if he suddenly found it too tight. 'Not always. I, er, I generally manage to come to some arrangement.'

I just bet you do, thought Rafferty. He forced himself to put aside all thoughts of the 'there but for the grace of' variety and pushed for answers. Anyway, he'd never liked euphemisms. He always preferred to get things nice and clear. 'Bungs, you mean? Cash payments and backhanders to the accountant, manager or whoever has responsibility for office maintenance? To whoever's able to authorize such cash payments and is willing to do so without asking a lot of difficult questions? Is that the arrangement you usually come to?'

Arnold's gaze moved shiftily between them. But it was apparent he expected no understanding from Llewellyn and he fastened on Rafferty's more charitable mien. However, it seemed Arnold wasn't prepared to commit himself to the folly of a verbal answer even to Rafferty. He restricted himself to a silent, hands widespread, 'What can you do?' gesture.

Rafferty tapped the card-index box. 'How are you doing on the details of your staff? Has your memory come back yet?'

Arnold nodded miserably. His easy smile had by now inexplicably vanished. As, no doubt, had half Arnold's illegal workforce once they'd heard about the murder.

119

'Good. I shall also need a list of your previous staff. And that means all of them; permanent, casuals, come-day-go-days, illegals, moonlighters, dole cheats, the lot. Any that ever worked at Aimhurst and Son or for Watts and Cutley or any of their subsidiaries. How many would that cover?'

'A few,' Arnold admitted.

'How many's a few?' demanded Llewellyn. 'Five? Six? Ten?'

Arnold waxed indignant. 'Certainly not that many. I only got the Aimhurst contract a few months ago and I've never supplied any workers to Watts and Cutley.'

'However many there are, we want their details.' After he had thrust a pen into Arnold's hand and watched him get started, Rafferty reasoned that any one of them could have talked their way past Albert Smith. Any one of them might have been sacked by Barstaple in the past; this would often be the line of work they'd end up in. He recalled he'd had doubts about Ada Collins, who had denied ever meeting Clive Barstaple. Now he asked Arnold what he knew of her.

Arnold paused mid-scribble. Out of all Arnold's workforce, it seemed that Ada Collins was one of the honest ones. She even declared her earnings to the taxman, Arnold confided. 'I inherited her when I bought the business,' he explained. 'She'd worked for my predecessor for years. Why do you want to know about her, particularly?' he asked, apparently feeling now that he'd been so helpful and all that he was entitled to ask a few questions. Suddenly, he grinned. 'Don't tell me you suspect Honest Ada of murder? That would be a turn-up.'

Rafferty declined to share the joke. 'We've already got the current addresses for Eric Penn, Ada Collins and Mrs Chakraburty, so why don't we start with Dot Flowers and go on from there?' Aware that he might not get a second chance, Rafferty was determined to stay until he got the information he wanted.

Ross Arnold scowled. 'I'm trying, aren't I?' He sat back. 'It's no good. I can't remember. Anyway, even if I could, she wouldn't be at home. According to Ada Collins, she went up to Birmingham to nursemaid her sick son. I don't expect her back this week.'

Or next week or any time at all, Rafferty silently tacked on. It was evident that Arnold would be surprised if he saw either Mrs Flowers or Mrs Chakraburty again. Such interest in them by any form of authority was not something such casual workers would relish.

'You must have a contact number, man.'

Arnold began to flip through his card-index box. He frowned and his flipping became increasingly anxious.

'Don't tell me,' said Rafferty. 'Her index card's not there. What a surprise.'

Apparently it was a surprise to Arnold as well. He had started to sweat, Rafferty noticed. Great dark patches had appeared under his meaty arms and his forehead glistened like morning dew.

Grabbing the box from him, Rafferty checked for himself. Neither Mrs Flowers' nor Mrs Chakraburty's cards were there. Guessing that a man like Arnold would find a good memory an asset, he suggested it would be in his interest to employ it. 'If not, I'm sure the Social and the Immigration people would be only too willing to help you remember those contact numbers.' Not to mention the Inland Revenue, Customs and Excise and the Council Business Tax bods.

It appeared that Arnold wouldn't need their assistance after all. He remembered the women's contact numbers with no problem at all. They were probably used by a number of his workers; such things got passed around.

Rafferty smiled. He hadn't been keen to seek the help of other government departments. He didn't want them tramping all over his investigation if he could help it. Fortunately, Arnold didn't know that.

'You said you only got the contract at Aimhurst's a short time ago,' Llewellyn broke in. 'How long ago, exactly?'

'Three months.'

Rafferty raised his eyebrows and commented, 'Interesting. That's when Clive Barstaple started there.'

Arnold said nothing.

'He was a friend of yours, I take it?'

'Hardly a friend.' Arnold was becoming shifty again. 'More an acquaintance. A business acquaintance.'

'And did you have one of your little arrangements with Clive Barstaple at Aimhurst's?' Rafferty asked.

Arnold was quick to deny it. But Rafferty had been expecting the denial and he didn't miss the brief spurt of alarm in Arnold's shifty hazel eyes. He would want to distance himself as much as he could from the murder victim. He was already far too close for comfort and being implicated in crooked deals with the dead man wasn't likely to decrease the proximity.

Rafferty suspected that Arnold might find it convenient to do another flit pretty soon. He wasn't too worried about that. Of course, he'd have to be checked out, but somehow he didn't think Arnold likely to go in for murder; certainly not that of someone like Barstaple. Arnold would prefer his victims to be weak and vulnerable like his illegal casual workers and no one – apart possibly from Llewellyn – could call Barstaple either.

Still, Rafferty took the time to take a statement from him as to his whereabouts on Wednesday and warned him he'd be watched so not to think of leaving town.

Though he doubted Arnold would be taken in by such a warning for long. A man who worked on the wrong side of half a dozen laws would soon realize police funds didn't stretch to such twenty-four-hour watches. But he was hopeful that Arnold wouldn't detect the lack of a tail till they'd checked his alibi.

'What an appalling man,' Llewellyn burst out when they were in the car and on their way back to the station.

Rafferty was surprised that Llewellyn hadn't found some easy excuse for Arnold's less pleasant character traits. After all, he'd managed to excuse Barstaple's with little difficulty. He glanced at Llewellyn and sighed when he saw that the Welshman was wearing his po-faced moral look.

'To think he's probably been running that business under our noses for months, flouting the law and getting away with it.'

Usually, Llewellyn kept his personal feelings out of an investigation, but it seemed he'd decided to make an exception in Ross Arnold's case. Rafferty soon learned why.

'If there's one thing I find contemptible it's people who think the law's only for others to obey. And like Arnold, they're generally full of mealy-mouthed excuses for their behaviour.'

Rafferty slunk down in his seat and just managed to swallow the groan. It was the first time Llewellyn had expressed such an opinion. Wasn't it just his luck, he thought, that Llewellyn's particular hobby horse should be the very thing that brought him most grief.

Few of Rafferty's family considered buying iffy 'bargains' a crime, and they indulged in such purchases frequently. His ma, unfortunately, had a particular weakness in this regard and refused to give it up no matter how much or how often he pleaded with her to do so. On the contrary, she always defended her actions vigorously. Every time he had reminded her that she was breaking the law, she had pooh-poohed him and told him that he should be out catching real criminals instead of browbeating his poor defenceless mother.

If only he could have confessed Ma's little failings to Llewellyn. But his sergeant had put the kibosh on that all right. To do such a thing now would be asking for trouble. After his outburst on morality, Llewellyn might feel it his duty to shop Ma. And if he did, who was to say what might not be the outcome? It wouldn't surprise him if she decided to come clean and bring a load of previous to be taken into consideration into the equation.

The merest suspicion of wrongdoing could be enough to wreck his and Llewellyn's careers. And the iffy suit provided a damn sight more than mere suspicion. It would certainly be enough for Superintendent Bradley to throw the book at him. Bradley would think his numbers had come up on the national lottery; it was unlikely he would stop at charging Ma with receiving. Before he finished, he'd have the entire Rafferty clan implicated and in the charge room.

Rafferty, never good at concealing his feelings at the best of times, had made little enough effort at hiding his contempt for his superintendent and his brown-nosing at Region. It was unfortunate that Bradley had finally sussed that the pleasingly apt acronym Rafferty had supplied last year for the Super's latest public relations scam – Politeness in Interaction with Members of the Public – PIMP for short – had been far from accidental.

But what did he expect when his public relations efforts

were only done to save money? The trouble was, of course, that being made to look a prat was unlikely to encourage the quality of mercy in the Super. More likely it would bring the quality of insistence on the pound of flesh to the fore.

Llewellyn, tarred with the brush of being his partner, could expect no mercy either. But then, for once, he didn't seem all that keen on dishing it out. Like a hell-fire preacher, he was still pounding Rafferty's ears from the pulpit of the passenger seat.

'That man should be exposed to the authorities, the Inland Revenue, for instance. If only to make it more difficult for him to set up his grubby business elsewhere.'

Rafferty nodded absently and abandoned any idea of confessing Ma's sins to Llewellyn. The penance would obviously be more than a few Hail Marys. With Plan A out of the running, he'd better concentrate on finding a Plan B and fast. His options weren't the only things that were rapidly reducing. Time wasn't on his side either.

The address given by Mrs Chakraburty proved to be false. On investigating the contact numbers supplied by Ross Arnold they discovered they belonged to corner shops; presumably their owners made additional income from providing message services for the local illegals and dole cheats.

And although Rafferty pressed them, he had to accept that the Asian families who ran the stores knew little more about either Mrs Chakraburty or Mrs Flowers than he did. All he did know was that the women usually popped in once or twice a day to see if they had any messages about work. As there seemed to be little chance that either woman would be stupid enough to continue to do so, it was a dead end, though he warned the shopkeepers concerned to let him know if either woman showed up.

He was hopeful that Birmingham would have more luck in tracing Mrs Flowers, at least. With any luck, her troublesome son was going to cause her even more problems by making her inconveniently accessible. As for Mrs Chakraburty, Rafferty suspected they had seen the last of her.

Arnold had insisted that, apart from Mrs Chakraburty and the several cleaners who had let him down right at the beginning of the contract, the cleaners at Aimhurst's had all worked there for most, if not all, of the three months he had held the contract. Only Dot Flowers had started later.

Rafferty, disinclined to believe anything the man said, intended to check Arnold's story with the two workers who remained – Ada Collins and Eric Penn. He half hoped Arnold had been telling fibs. It would be some satisfaction to haul the man into the station and give him a proper grilling.

Meanwhile, unable to stop scratching at the scab, as they got back in the car after questioning the last shopkeeper, Rafferty glanced across at Llewellyn and asked, 'How's Maureen's mother getting on with those wedding lists, then? All done?'

Llewellyn gave a tiny moue. 'I'm afraid not. Unfortunately, my future mother-in-law's trouble is that she doesn't know when to stop. Maureen and I are going over there tonight to try to make her see that a grand reception for four hundred is out of the question.'

The normally imperturbable Welshman had a decidedly hunted look. Rafferty felt a tiny spasm of guilt that he should be pleased this wedding was causing problems for someone other than himself. Llewellyn's repressed personality and Methodist upbringing would, he was sure, find the thought of such excess thoroughly distasteful.

Llewellyn had the bit firmly between his compressed lips. 'She seems determined to turn this into the wedding of the year. Maureen rang again before we left the station and told me the guest list is now completely out of hand. I don't know who her mother thinks is going to pay for it all. It's some consolation, I suppose, that they won't all accept. According to Maureen, we've already received our first firm refusals. She said her mother was really put out by one or two. Especially those from Mr and Mrs Empson-Palmer, Mrs Toogood, and . . .'

Rafferty tuned his mind out from the listing of the great and the good at this point. He had scratched the scab and now wished he hadn't. By the sound of it the revelations of Ma's misdeeds would have a large audience.

Five minutes later he pulled into the station car park, parked the car across two bays and strode, grim-faced, towards the offices. He had a lot to fit in this morning. First, he had to read the reports that had come in during their absence, then he had to write up his own reports. Lastly, he had another little visit to fit in, though this had nothing to do with the murder inquiry. It was entirely for his own private satisfaction.

Ten

Rafferty opened his ma's front door with his own key and slammed into the living room without bothering to shout, 'It's only me,' as he usually did.

He had startled her, he realized, as her dyed and permed dark head shot up. But any guilt was quickly squashed by a feeling of irritation. What did he have to feel guilty about? It was Ma who should be feeling guilt-ridden. But did she? Not her. She looked as innocent and butter-wouldn't-melt as the mythical white-haired granny she in no way resembled. Obviously untroubled by the Catholic conscience that gave him so much trouble, her plump body was surrounded by a halo of pure white as she knitted a romper suit for the expected great-grandchild.

'I suppose you've heard the news?' he demanded. 'That Llewellyn and Maureen have set the date for their wedding?'

She gave a satisfied nod. 'I have that. Isn't it just grand?' She put on the stern face that he remembered so well from childhood. 'And don't bang into the house like an enraged bull, Joseph. You know it's not good for my nerves.'

Rafferty wished he had nerves as robust. His were currently looking for bolt holes to crawl into.

Her bright blue eyes glanced at his worn brown suit much as Llewellyn had. 'I'm thinking you'll be wishing, now that it's too late, that you'd taken me up on that bargain suit I had for you at Christmas.'

Rafferty felt the gorge rise in his throat and he shouted, 'Don't mention bloody suits to me, Ma! I'm up to here with the damn things. You might have told me at the time that you had more than one, but oh no, you kept quiet. And why you had to sell the other one to Llewellyn, of all people . . . ! You know how po-faced he can be about dodgy gear. If anyone recognizes it—'

'You worry too much, son,' she told him complacently. With infuriating logic, she added, 'And I sold it to Dafyd because I knew it would fit him. Besides, a suit's a suit. It's not as if it's starred in one of those crime programmes on the telly.'

'No, but it's about to star at Llewellyn's wedding – with Superintendent Bradley as one of the audience. I shouldn't think we'll have long to wait before you, me, and the bridegroom do our own star turn – in the dock for receiving.'

The knitting needles paused momentarily, then started clicking fast and furious, so Rafferty was sure he had hit the spot. But he knew better than to expect either an apology or sympathy. Being made to feel guilty had always given Ma's tongue more stings than a nettlefield. This occasion was no exception.

'I told you you should have gone on the buildings like your da and brothers,' she observed with a tart disregard for the truth that almost took Rafferty's breath away, neatly turning the argument so his current predicament was his fault. 'But would you listen? No, not you. Had to be different. Had to be a policeman. Now look where it's got you.'

Ma had always had a natural gift for turning the facts on their heads when it suited her argument. It certainly wasn't how Rafferty remembered it and he protested, 'But it was you—' he began.

'That's right. Blame me.' Kitty Rafferty sniffed and wiped a non-existent tear from her eye. 'A poor widder woman, I was. Left all alone with six kids to bring up. Tried to do my best by you all. Did I get any thanks? No, of course I didn't. I never expected any, mothers never do. Many's the time you broke my heart. Many's the time you . . .'

As this was an all-too-familiar theme, Rafferty held up his hands in an attempt to halt the flow. 'All right, Ma. I'm obviously the world's most thoughtless, ungrateful son. I'm sorry. Jesus,' he muttered under his breath; he knew better than to say the word aloud, it would only start her off again. But it infuriated him that the apology had been forced from him rather than from her. It wasn't how it was meant to be. But somehow, Ma always seemed to get the better of him. Just once he wanted to win both the argument and the moral high ground.

He had meant to really lay it on the line to her that she had given him a major headache. But his encounter with Ross Arnold and his sweat-shop business ethics had weakened his resolve. It had reminded him of the many sacrifices she had made after his dad had died. He and his brothers and sisters had all still been young. He remembered some of the jobs Ma had taken; sewing in a sack factory; packing in a sweet factory; on her feet all day in all weathers on a market stall . . . But she'd still, somehow, found time to bake cakes and puddings. Still somehow managed to produce tasty meals from the cheapest ingredients.

He'd remembered, too, that even Ma's love of 'bargains' had sprung from the need to provide for them.

Endless money worries, desperation and sheer necess-
ity had forced her to buy dodgy gear, and working in
the market had placed her in the way of lots of such
merchandise. Nobody in their right mind would have
turned their noses up under such circumstances and Ma
had always been very practical. So how could he come
the heavy-handed son now, when desperation no longer
drove her purchases?

Feeling a complete heel – as no doubt crafty Kitty had
intended – he returned from his trip down memory lane
to find that at least his unwarranted apology had had the
desired effect and the knitting needles had slowed to a
more hypnotic rhythm. Rafferty, who had begun to feel
half-mesmerized by their eye-blurring speed, blinked and
broke the spell.

Although his ma would never admit to feeling guilty,
she did have the grace to look a little abashed. However,
she soon recovered and set about a sturdy defence.

'Anyway,' she asked. 'who's going to identify Llewellyn's suit if your superintendent does decide to ask
awkward questions? Sure and my tailor friend has taken
off now that the insurance has paid out, so he won't be
around to answer anybody's questions. I'd put it out of
your mind, son.'

It seemed she had. For now, she held up the half-
finished romper suit and said, 'What do you think? It's
a new pattern I'm trying, but my first great-grandchild
should have something special.'

Her quick recovery deflated any further impulse Rafferty
might have had to take her to task and he gazed with
lacklustre eyes from the suit she held up to the pattern. It
would certainly be fancy enough for little Lord Fauntleroy
himself when it was finished, he thought disgustedly. Not
only would it have satin quilting attached to the wrists

and chest, it would also, he noted, sport a big satin bow at the neck.

Its fancy-work brought home to him that his ma was taking the Great Granny Stakes even more seriously than his father had taken the Oaks, the Grand National and the Derby combined.

And he'd thought the Grandmother Cup important enough in her general scheme of things. With twelve grandchildren to her credit, Ma had won that by a furlong last year, leaving the rest of the neighbourhood grannies trailing. But this year, Mrs Thingy's daughter-in-law three doors down had had twins and Her Next Door's daughter had had triplets.

Ma had taken umbrage at this, insisting it was hardly sporting, especially as she hadn't even troubled to get a husband first. 'Calls herself "Mrs" Williams,' Ma had sniffed. 'She's not, of course. Occasionally she manages to drag the father round her mother's just to keep up the pretence for the neighbours. I don't know who she thinks she's fooling, as I know for a fact he's still living on All Saints Avenue with the real Mrs Williams.'

His ma knew all the street scandal and that of the area for a good half-mile round. His 'Uncle' Pat jokingly referred to her as the News of the World.

Rafferty felt an upsurge of his earlier irritation and was half-tempted to remind her that the object of her pride – the first great-grandchild, which was due in the summer – was also going to be born out of wedlock. But he thought better of it when he recalled how much the news had upset her. Ma had moral principles as high as Llewellyn's on some things and he didn't want a return of the upset and disappointment she'd suffered when she'd first learned of his niece Gemma's pregnancy, just before Christmas.

Rafferty's heart seemed to do another belly-flop dive

to the pit of his stomach as she brought up the subject closest to her heart. 'You're my eldest,' she reminded him, as if he needed telling. 'Just wait till you produce a son. If I have anything to do with it, he'll have six suits a day and ten for Sundays.'

But as there appeared no immediate likelihood of him producing a winning argument, never mind a son, even Ma had to accept the fact. Her next comment made clear that she didn't find this easy.

'Though I wish you'd get a move on. Her Next Door is always asking after you. "Has poor Joseph found himself a steady girlfriend yet?" is her favourite refrain.'

'Is it?' he asked shortly. He hadn't come here to listen to a lecture, he reminded himself. He'd come to give one. But, as usual, Ma had managed to twist things round to her advantage.

It was obvious that Her Next Door had annoyed Ma, because she dropped a stitch. With a 'Tshaw', she picked it up again before adding, 'It's always "Poor Joseph" with her, as though she thought there was something wrong with you.' She peered interrogatively up at him over her knitting. 'There's not, is there?'

Rafferty scowled. 'For God's sake, Ma! There's nothing the matter with me that staying out of the dock won't cure. And as for that old bat next door, why don't you just tell her I've set up a love-nest with the Archbishop of Canterbury next time she asks?'

His ma, the lover of iffy 'bargains', gazed disapprovingly at him over her new bifocals. 'I know you're upset, Joseph, but that's no reason to blaspheme.'

Ma thought the Church of England capable of anything and she certainly didn't approve of her son mentioning the name of their big chief in the same breath as that of the Almighty. In her opinion, the Church of England and the Almighty had little enough to do with one another as it was.

'For your information,' Rafferty told her, 'no, I haven't started dressing to the left in my old age, if that's what you're hinting at.'

Kitty Rafferty smiled and went back to her knitting. 'That's good, son. So I suppose I can look forward to you giving me a grandson sometime in the future?'

Rafferty's lips tightened. It was unfortunate for him that, in the Grandma Stakes, he was Ma's biggest handicap; an eleven-and-a-half-stone handicap. His two brothers were at least married, but he hadn't even got a filly lined up under starter's orders. Her Next Door, with her growing brood of grandchildren, was edging up on the stand side and looked set to overtake. No wonder she was starting to get under Ma's defences.

He was sorely tempted to remind her that Her Next Door would have something else to occupy her mind if – no, when – Superintendent Bradley sniffed out the truth about Llewellyn's wedding suit. And it wouldn't be when 'Poor Joseph' was going to get himself a steady girlfriend.

After a night filled with exhausting equestrian dreams saddled up and ridden hard for the finish by an over-exuberant jockey Ma, Rafferty overslept and woke to aching bones and the realization that, in addition to his other troubles, he'd somehow caught the flu. By the time he finally got to the station, he wasn't in the best of tempers. And the sight of a bright-eyed and bushy-tailed Llewellyn did nothing to improve his mood.

'How's that hunt for possible grudge-holders from Barstaple's past going?' he asked Llewellyn. 'Found any matches yet with Aimhurst's or Watts and Cutley's employees?'

Contrarily, he half-hoped for a negative reply; it would give him the excuse he needed to have a moan. After all, he reasoned, it was Llewellyn's peculiar combination of high morals, low vanity, and naivety that had helped put him in his current fix. With anybody else, he could have just told them the suit was iffy and to get rid and that would be that. Not with Llewellyn, of course. With him, everything always turned out to be as complicated as one of Ma's knitting patterns. He wasn't surprised when Llewellyn even managed to frustrate his modest, if unreasonable, desire to find fault.

'Actually, we've turned up quite a number of grudge-holders,' Llewellyn loftily replied. 'Though none with any connection with Watts and Cutley or Aimhurst's – or, at least, none that we have so far been able to discover.'

'What? Not even a relief deliveryman or two?'

'You're not still yearning after a murdering milkman, are you, sir?' Llewellyn asked, raising his eyebrows and gazing at him in that superior schoolmasterly manner that made Rafferty feel even more irritated.

'No, not really.' He collapsed into his chair. In spite of his bad mood, bad head, and aching bones, Rafferty managed a grin. 'But it has a certain poetic charm which I thought would appeal to you.'

'Indeed.' Llewellyn's po-face all but told him that he, for one, kept his poetical yearnings well away from his police work. 'Apart from an irritating tendency to off-key whistling, our particular dairymen appear totally blameless.'

Rafferty nodded, sneezed loudly and slumped over his desk as Llewellyn continued.

'Lilley and I did think we'd got something earlier; a

young man Barstaple sacked two firms ago who was known to have threatened him. This chap, Anderson, actually worked as a cleaner for Ross Arnold for a while and even did a couple of stints at Aimhurst and Son's offices not long before Mrs Flowers replaced him.'

Rafferty stopped rummaging around in his desk for painkillers long enough to ask, 'So, what's come of it?'

'Nothing. This particular chap, Michael Anderson, hadn't turned up for work for several days – this is the best part of three months ago – and hasn't been seen since. We discovered he died in the Midlands just after new year.'

Rafferty frowned. 'You're sure it was him?' It wasn't that he doubted Llewellyn's findings; far from it, whatever else he might be the Welshman was a competent policeman. But he couldn't help asking. 'There was a positive ID?'

Llewellyn nodded. 'His landlord identified him. Besides, he had a record and the prints matched. There was no doubt about it, according to the Midlands police, who checked the matter out. It seems, from what they found in his room, that Anderson had become something of a drifter since Barstaple sacked him from his last proper job; there were bus tickets and store receipts from all over the country. It was the usual story, I gather; depression, self-neglect, self-abuse and death. But whatever else he might have been, he definitely wasn't Barstaple's murderer.' Llewellyn paused. 'As for the other firms Barstaple worked for, so far we've not turned up any other possibles, but it's slow going and—'

Rafferty broke in. 'OK, I get the picture. Look, I didn't realize when I asked you to check out the employees of the firms that Barstaple freelanced for that there'd be quite so many of them. I suggest you let Lilley continue on his own.'

136

Llewellyn nodded. 'By the way, remember you asked me to check with Birmingham about Mrs Flowers' son? According to the officer who checked the matter out for me, nobody by the name of Flowers was admitted to any of Birmingham's hospitals in the last two weeks. No one of that name had been admitted to any of the hospitals in the surrounding areas either. The difficulty is, of course, that her son might have a different name.'

Rafferty nodded. 'I should think it's almost certain he has. Why should Dot Flowers be any different from the rest of Ross Arnold's workforce? Damn the man. Him and his illegals and dole cheats are adding an unnecessary complication to this case.'

'Do you want me to put a trace out for Mrs Flowers? I should be able to get a good description from Mrs Collins and Ross Arnold.'

Rafferty agreed. 'Get them down the station to work on a photofit. Do Mrs Chakraburty at the same time. At least we know what she looks like, so hers can be circulated immediately. We'll hold fire on circulating Mrs Flowers' photofit, though. Birmingham could turn her up at any time and, if her son is in hospital, I don't want to cause her any unnecessary grief. Besides, first I want to check if she was really called Flowers. There can't be that many people with the name in the area.'

According to DC Hanks, to whom Rafferty had allocated the job of checking, there were six Flowers in the phone book, and the same number on the electoral roll. Again, according to Hanks, none of them were dark, female or over sixty.

Rafferty was pondering his next move and forcing an

Alka Seltzer down his throat when Llewellyn returned with the news that the two photofits that Rafferty had requested had been organized.

'Better get the one of Mrs Flowers circulated as well now.' Rafferty advised Llewellyn of Hanks' poor luck in connecting her with any of the locals of that name. Birmingham still had no answers. 'Is Lilley in, do you know?'

'He's in the CID room working on those lists of Barstaple's previous firms.'

'Tell him I want to see him, will you? I want to find out how he's getting on.'

Unfortunately, Lilley, young and keen, was no more able to speed up the time-consuming checking for Barstaple's old enemies than Llewellyn had been.

Since setting himself up as an independent consultant, Barstaple had rarely stayed longer than three months with any one firm. This, of course, meant that the list of his possible enemies was long. It also meant that in between Barstaple rationalizing them in a previous job, and their possibly being taken on by Watts and Cutley or any of their subsidiaries, his would-be murderer could have married or changed their recognizability quotient in any number of ways.

Barstaple wouldn't necessarily recognize an old adversary, in any event. If his killer was employed in the head office and made a point of keeping his head down, only visiting Aimhurst's after checking that Barstaple was absent, he might not have had the opportunity.

It wasn't even as if they could concentrate on those who had joined Watts and Cutley after Barstaple; it could be that his murderer had already been in post when he had been hired as their axe-wielding consultant. His hiring would undoubtedly bring with it a return of

138

all the bitterness and resentment felt at the time of their rationalization at their old firm.

Watts and Cutley's business interests were extremely diverse and their employees ran into the thousands. Checking them all out for possible past links with Barstaple would take for ever. It was one of the reasons Rafferty had pulled Llewellyn off the job and given it to Lilley. Along with the lists and the visitors' book, he had given him the instruction to do the job as quickly as he could, but most of all, to be thorough. That was exactly what he was being, Rafferty discovered. If only it wasn't so painfully slow.

It was Friday evening and Llewellyn returned from getting the circulation of Mrs Flowers' photofit organized to learn that forensic had finished at Aimhurst's offices and things were back to normal. Or at least as normal as they could be after a murder.

Forensic had found little of interest. Admittedly, they had found fingerprints on the pot of hazelnut yoghurt in Barstaple's wastebin, but the only prints on it were those of the victim himself and his milkman. There were a few other, smudged ones, but they were insufficient to be of any value. Certainly, there were no matches with any of their more obvious suspects, who had all been fingerprinted as a matter of course.

Llewellyn consulted his watch and remarked, 'It seems an ideal opportunity to put Albert Smith's hearing to the test. The staff won't start back to work till Monday and the cleaners won't have arrived, so we'll be able to stage the test under the same quiet conditions that would have applied just before the time of Barstaple's death.'

Made wretched by the flu, Rafferty had forgotten all

about this test, but now he rallied, stretched and stood up. 'I wanted to have another word with Ada Collins, too, so we'll be able to kill two birds with one stone. Let's get over there.'

Eleven

W hen Rafferty and Llewellyn reached Aimhurst's
offices it was about 5.45 p.m. Rafferty had thought
Albert Smith would be the only one there, but, as they
walked up the side of the drive, having left the car on the
road, he was surprised to see Marian Steadman through
the reception window.

She and Smith appeared to be having an argument.
Their dark heads were thrust forward either side of the
reception desk, and their waving hands made the same
emphatic gestures. This silent, apparently mimed argument looked curiously comical. They reminded Rafferty
of a particular bonus VCRs conferred; the ability to play
the more pompous politicians in reverse so they looked
like marionettes gone mad. It never failed to give him
a good belly laugh. In her heyday, Maggie Thatcher had
been a favourite for this treatment; she hadn't seemed
nearly so formidable when she'd been zapped backwards
through the cathode ray tube.

Marian Steadman and Albert Smith were apparently so
absorbed in their discussion that they didn't notice when
Rafferty pressed the latest entry code on the keypad by
the front door and entered reception with Llewellyn just
behind him.

They heard Marian Steadman say, 'I know very well
you've been avoiding me. You can't deny you must

have—' She broke off as Smith threw her a warning glance. The pair sprang apart guiltily and two pairs of dark eyes fastened on Rafferty with matching expressions of dismay.

The two policemen exchanged bemused glances. What was that about? Rafferty wondered. The pair seemed – conspiratorial. It was the only word to describe their behaviour. Yet he couldn't imagine a more unlikely pair of conspirators. Marian Steadman's dark eyes were intelligent, warm, humorous. Smith's were none of these things; even his pepper and salt moustache had a downward cast as if it shared its owner's outlook on the world. Rafferty could only think Marian Steadman felt sorry for him.

Marian Steadman was the first to recover her poise. 'Hello, Inspector,' she said. 'You startled me.' She made no attempt to explain the argument, which, to Rafferty, either pushed her intelligence up a notch or confirmed her innocence of any misdeed. 'I thought you'd finished examining the offices.'

'We have,' Rafferty confirmed. 'Don't let us disturb you,' he added. They didn't take him up on his invitation. 'We're just going upstairs for a minute.'

Marian Steadman buttoned her coat and said, 'I was just going, anyway. See you Monday, Albert. Have a nice weekend.' She bid them adieu and disappeared.

Rafferty and Llewellyn rounded the bend and climbed the stairs to the first floor. They waited till, through the main office window, they saw Marian Steadman reach the forecourt entrance, turn right and head out of sight up the main road and then Llewellyn vanished into the gent's toilet while Rafferty concealed himself behind the door of the open-plan office.

He had no difficulty hearing Llewellyn's shout for help. Neither, it appeared, did Albert Smith. He came racing up the stairs, two at a time, and burst into the lavatory, displaying a zeal for assisting the police that Rafferty found commendable. He only hoped it continued when they questioned him.

'What's going on?' the security man demanded of the loitering Llewellyn when he found him apparently unharmed. 'I thought someone was being murder—' He stopped abruptly. Then, belatedly realizing that there must be more to this than he understood, he tightened his lips and stared mulishly at Llewellyn.

Rafferty popped his head round the door and commented, 'I see there's nothing wrong with your hearing, Mr Smith. Perhaps you can explain why you didn't hear Clive Barstaple shout for help? I think he must have shouted, don't you? More than once, too. He must have been in agony, unable to help himself and desperate. Surely you heard him?'

Rafferty's insistence that he must have done so made Smith surly and defensive. 'Maybe he didn't shout at all,' he told them. 'But even if he did, I didn't hear him. Got my rounds to do, haven't I? Must have done any shouting while I was at the other end of the building checking the place was secure.'

It was plausible, Rafferty had to concede. Smith must be smarter than he looked. He had certainly come up with a defence quickly enough.

'And what time, exactly, do you do your rounds, Mr Smith?' Llewellyn asked.

Smith paused a moment before answering. Probably doing some swift mental arithmetic was Rafferty's suspicious conclusion. 'Around half-five or just after.'

'And how long would your rounds generally take?'

Smith shifted his feet and scowled, but he admitted to fifteen minutes.

'Did you check in Barstaple's office at all?'

Smith apparently now felt brave enough to scoff at Llewellyn's question. 'Of course not. I knew he was still there, didn't I? Wouldn't have thanked me if I'd disturbed him.'

'You know that for sure, do you, Mr Smith?' Llewellyn asked. 'We understand Mr Barstaple had something of a reputation for being unpleasant. Had you had a run in with him at all?'

A brief shadow passed across Smith's features and was as quickly gone. 'No. No need. I do my job properly. I've had no complaints.'

Llewellyn didn't pursue it. 'What about the toilets? Did you check them?'

Llewellyn's gaze was steady, unthreatening, but Smith avoided it. 'No. The windows in there don't open. There was no point in checking them.'

Rafferty raised an eyebrow. So much for Smith's claim that he did his job properly. Now he took over the questioning. 'Surely you must have been instructed to check everywhere, particularly in view of the recent threats against the firm. Besides, you couldn't be sure one of our local hooligans hadn't smashed a window in one of the toilets. We had reports of a gang of youths causing trouble out this way that night.'

'The windows are still there, aren't they? Besides, I'd have heard it smash.'

'Even if you were at the other end of the building? You can't be certain of that,' Rafferty insisted. 'After all, you didn't hear Clive Barstaple shout.'

'Glass is different. It makes a much sharper sound. The noise would have carried. Besides,' he repeated, 'we none of us know that he *did* shout.'

Rafferty was half-tempted to put Smith's theory to the

test and smash a pane of glass at the rear of the premises. But the thought of explaining such vandalism to
Bradley and Alistair Plumley made him forget the idea.
Why court more problems? But there was one thing he
could try smashing – Smith's claim to innocence. There
was something decidedly shifty in the man's manner.
And once the security man had returned to his duties
downstairs, Rafferty instructed Llewellyn to get back on
to Guardian Security, Smith's employers, to see if they
could tell them any more about the man than the basics
they had so far supplied.

Downstairs once more, they ignored Smith's sullen face
and settled in the staff room to await the arrival of the
cleaners.

'I can't believe that Barstaple didn't make some attempt
to get help,' Llewellyn commented as Rafferty studied the
drinks machine and hunted in his pocket for change.

'Nor me.' Rafferty broke off. 'Oh good, they've got
vegetable soup.' He hoped something warming in his
stomach would persuade his bones to stop aching. 'After
all, Barstaple's phone was dangling over the edge of the
desk so it seems likely he tried to summon outside help.
Maybe that's because he'd given up on getting any of the
other sort. He must have been in that lavatory for some
time, far longer than the fifteen minutes that Smith claims
his rounds take. Which leaves us with the probability that
Smith did hear him, but chose to ignore him.' He gazed
speculatively at Llewellyn. 'Any ideas as to why?'

Llewellyn hadn't. Rafferty turned back to the drinks
machine, inserted his coins and made his selection.
Nothing happened. He thumped the machine, but this
brought no result either and he scowled. 'Blasted thing.
Bet you it won't give me my money back, either.'

However, to his surprise, the machine proved more

honest than most of its breed and regurgitated his coins once Llewellyn suggested he press the reject button. The noise of a vacuum cleaner starting up told him the cleaners had arrived earlier than he had expected and he decided to abandon the idea of soup. It was as well to quit while he was ahead.

They went out to the reception area. At the desk, Albert Smith's head was determinedly bent over some papers. Rafferty ignored him. For the moment he had other things on his mind than the security guard's suspiciously selective deafness and he went in search of Ada Collins. Even if she had found Mrs Chakraburty no more chatty than he had, the Asian woman might have let slip something about her family to another woman. Dot Flowers had done so, after all. Rafferty felt that if he could just find the two women, who were presumably working illegally, he might be in a position to eliminate them from the inquiry. There was enough to do without chasing around trying to find people who were probably guilty of nothing more than working off the books. Besides, with his body laid low with flu and half his mind occupied with personal problems, he was having trouble enough keeping on top of it all. On top of the inquiry was the last thing he felt.

After walking round a mop and bucket wielded enthusiastically by Eric Penn on the reception area floor, Rafferty followed the noise of the electric cleaner to its source in one of the downstairs offices. It was there that he found Ada Collins.

She switched off the cleaner as soon as she saw them. 'I wondered if I'd see you again. Ross Arnold's been complaining you've scared off half his workers. I've even been able to get a pay rise out of him.' Her smile became conspiratorial. 'You must have put the wind up him good and proper.'

Absolute Poison

'All in the line of duty,' Rafferty told her. He propped himself on the edge of a desk, surprised that Ross Arnold hadn't yet staged his own disappearing act. Arnold's business must be even more lucrative than he had imagined.

'About time somebody did,' she remarked. 'The way he treats the likes of Eric and those poor Asian women is sinful.' She shrugged. 'All right I know they're illegals and not supposed to be in the country, never mind working, but they're decent, hard-working people, most of them. You can't help feeling sorry for them. A few of the women I've worked with have told me they felt they had no chance of any kind of a life in their own countries, so they come here, hoping for better. Fat chance of that when they have to work for the likes of Arnold. Sad little things, some of them.'

Rafferty nodded. He could imagine Ross Arnold would be the type to enjoy bullying people who couldn't fight back. 'I gather Arnold had a few other people working here at the beginning of the contract.' He already knew about Anderson and now he questioned her about the others.

'Not much I can tell you,' she said. 'They came, worked a few days and then left.' Mrs Collins screwed up her forehead. 'If I remember rightly there were three, all told; two Asian women and one white chap. I haven't seen any of them since. None of them was much more than thirty. Told me their first names and nothing else. Then Dot Flowers started shortly after the new year and we were more settled.'

Curious, Rafferty asked, 'Why do you choose to work for a man like Arnold?'

She shrugged. 'I just stayed on when he bought the business. Not one for change, me. Though I was surprised he let me stay, given the set-up he prefers. But I'm reliable, you see. I suppose that's what stopped him

147

getting rid of me. With the illegals he employs, he can never be sure when they'll feel it necessary to move on and leave him shorthanded, so he has to have a few old faithfuls.'

'Tell me about Mrs Chakraburty. You know she's disappeared?'

Ada Collins nodded. 'Ross Arnold told me I'd likely be getting another replacement. Can't say I'm surprised.'

'Had you worked with her before?'

'No. This was the first time. And the last, I imagine.

Rafferty had hoped for more. 'I take it then that you didn't know her well?'

'I doubt anyone ever gets the chance to know her well. She hardly opened her mouth the few evenings she worked with me and just did what I directed her to do. And, of course, her English wasn't too good. Like all of them, she was between the devil and the deep blue sea. Although I didn't get to know her, I've known plenty of women like her. Men too, though it's mostly women I see. They all knew well enough that they had no rights. Knew they had to take whatever the likes of Ross Arnold dished out. They stuck it because they had no alternative.'

'So you've no idea where she lived or what her real name is?'

'I'm afraid not. As I said, she didn't talk about herself. I barely knew the woman.'

'What about Mrs Flowers? You told my sergeant you thought she was foreign. Do you think she was an illegal, too?'

Ada Collins frowned. 'I'm not sure. It was more an impression I had, as if she was somewhere else half the time.' She shrugged. 'Most of them are. It was that more than anything that made me think she might be foreign. But I have to say that she spoke English as plain as you or me. Some of them do. Educated, some of them, and use this sort of work as a stopgap.'

'Have you heard from her since she phoned you?' Llewellyn asked.

She shook her head. 'No. Not a word since last Friday night. Still, I expect with her son in hospital, she's got more to worry about than keeping Ross Grab-it-all Arnold sweet. Jobs like this are ten a penny. She can get another one easily enough when she comes back. There are no shortage of employers of Ross Arnold's stamp.' She paused and then added, 'If she comes back, that is. She'll have heard of the murder here by now, so she may decide she can do without getting tangled up in it.'

'We've contacted various hospitals in Birmingham,' Llewellyn butted in. 'But none of them had admitted a male named Flowers. Of course, it's possible that's not his name, especially if Mrs Flowers is working here illegally and using a false name, but I wanted to check that you're sure she said Birmingham.'

Rafferty hadn't considered that possibility and he looked sharply at Ada Collins. Her look of doubt didn't inspire confidence.

She apologized. 'I *thought* she said Birmingham, but now you mention it I can't be sure. It was a bad line,' she explained, 'and I couldn't hear her all that well. It's not as if I thought it was important. It certainly began with a "B" and ended with a "ham". It's the bit in the middle I'm not sure of.'

'You're at least fairly confident that this place name is a three syllable word?' Llewellyn asked. Ada Collins looked blankly at him and he explained. 'Birmingham makes *three* distinctly separate sounds. Are you sure the name Mrs Flowers mentioned had the same?'

Ada Collins shook her head and told him apologetically,

'I can't be sure. I'm sorry. Dot Flowers had a coughing spasm while she was talking to me and the middle part of the name was obliterated by her spluttering. It didn't help that there was some sort of echo on the line.'

Rafferty stifled a groan. He even managed a faint smile when Ada Collins said encouragingly, 'Still, there can't be that many place names beginning with a "B" and ending with a "ham". It should be easy enough to check.' He hoped she was right. He thanked her for her help and the unwelcome information and they left her to her work. With witnesses and possible suspects disappearing at the rate they were, this case was rapidly turning into an Agatha Christie saga. He could only hope his suspects didn't continue to disappear 'until there were none' as had the characters in Mrs Christie's famous novel.

Twelve

With his mind still wrestling with the suit problem and his body plagued by what seemed to be turning into a particularly virulent form of influenza, Rafferty was finding it increasingly difficult to summon the energy to give the inquiry the lead it demanded. Llewellyn wasn't similarly troubled and he had apparently decided he had to take the initiative. He took to it like a duck to water.

Rafferty let him get on with it. After all, if he didn't manage to come up with a solution to the wedding suit problem it might be the only taste of rank and responsibility Llewellyn got.

Llewellyn had checked out the NHS website for a listing of all the hospitals in the country as well as using various search engines to check on possible place names. Not satisfied with these, he was currently working his efficient way through various atlases and gazetteers checking on place names that began with 'B' and ended with 'ham'. He had already collected quite an impressive list, Rafferty noted. But, if they were to eliminate Mrs Flowers from the inquiry, they had no choice but to check with the hospitals of each place on the list. He knew he should be grateful that Llewellyn had not only thought of the possibility that Mrs Collins had misheard the name of the place where Mrs Flowers' son was hospitalized, but had also taken upon himself the responsibility of following it up. He wasn't, of course. And his conscience, which, like him, had been subdued of late, bestirred itself sufficiently to tell him he was an ingrate.

Pausing to wipe his streaming nose, Rafferty peered over Llewellyn's shoulder. Burnham, Bookham, Brookham, he read. And Beckenham, Balham, Balcome, Bulphan, Burham . . . He drew back with a sigh when he saw that Llewellyn's growing list still scarcely extended beyond the Greater London area.

'I presume we're doing this phonetically as well as alphabetically?' Llewellyn asked.

'What?'

'Balcome isn't spelt "ham" at the end, but it sounds as if it is and Bulphan is also pretty close.'

'I suppose so.' Rafferty waved his hand over the list of names. 'You don't think this is a total waste of time?'

'Probably. But it looks worse than it is. Most of the smaller places won't even have hospitals, so will be quickly eliminated. But we've got to check.'

'I know that.' Rafferty paused, then burst out, 'But do you have to be the one to do all this? It's taking far too much time. We're neglecting our more likely suspects; the staff of Aimhurst's. We haven't even got around to asking Hal Gallagher about the argument he's supposed to have had with Barstaple yet. Maybe we're wrong to become so obsessed with a couple of off-the-books cleaners who weren't even on the payroll at Aimhurst's.'

Rafferty thought of all the other checking that was still to be done and felt more ill and depressed than ever. 'I could use your help checking them out, not in doing glorified clerical work.'

For once, mercifully, Llewellyn didn't pull him up by pointing out the obvious – that if he had been doing any such checking he'd kept it very quiet. Instead, in a long-suffering voice, he asked, 'Who do you suggest replaces me? Smales?'

Rafferty didn't even bother to answer that one. He tried and failed to come up with the name of one officer who could not only be spared for the task, but who could be relied upon to be as painstaking as Llewellyn. Half of them spelt even worse than Rafferty himself and would be likely to miss half of the possible sound-alike names.

'I don't know why you've got such a bee in your bonnet about those blasted lists, anyway,' he complained, and repeated, 'it's not as if we haven't got enough else to do.'

'It's just that I've a feeling,' Llewellyn told him.

'A feeling? You?' Weakened by flu and self-pity, this was too much for Rafferty and before he went on he had to subside into a chair. 'Since when has Llewellyn the Logical let feelings lead him by the nose? Let me give you a bit of advice,' he continued. 'You stick to logic and leave the feelings to me and Smales. And as for those lists.' He made a disgusted noise in the back of his throat. 'Just don't bother me with any feelings you might have about them. I don't want to know. And you needn't think you're going to spend all your time playing word games. You can have half an hour a day till next Wednesday and then we'll see.'

Stiff-necked, Rafferty strode to the door, consulted his watch and said, 'You've got thirty minutes, then I want you to come with me to see, first Bob Harris's wife and then Hal Gallagher before they go out for the evening. We've been sidetracked on these damn illegals long enough. I, for one, think it's high time we found out more about the main suspects. First, if his wife had given Harris an ultimatum and whether he believed she meant it.

'And second, what story Hal Gallagher has come up

with to convince us that his argument with Barstaple wasn't a prelude to murder.' After these self-righteous pronouncements, Rafferty stamped out, muttering 'feelings' to himself as he banged the door behind him.

Rafferty was surprised to see that Eileen Harris still displayed her wedding photos on the living-room cabinet. He would have expected them to be packed away along with the wreck of her marriage.

'How full of hope and optimism we were, Inspector,' she commented as she caught the direction of his gaze. 'How young and stupid.'

They had certainly looked the first three of those things, Rafferty thought as he studied the happy faces of the young couple as they smiled into each other's eyes. Tragically, life had in the intervening years succeeded in transforming hope into disappointment, optimism into despair, and – in Eileen Harris's case at least – youth into middle-aged cynicism. The sweetly smiling mouth in the photograph was now surrounded by lines of bitterness.

But as the disappointments of life, marriage, and everything, were too close to home for comfort, Rafferty was not inclined to dwell on them. He cleared his sore throat and said, 'We're here about the murder of your husband's boss, Clive Barstaple. You're aware he was found murdered on Wednesday evening?'

She nodded, but made no other comment.

'Your husband—'

Impatiently, she brushed back her dull brown hair and broke in, 'Estranged husband, Inspector.'

'Your estranged husband,' he corrected, 'told me you and he had a lunch appointment on Wednesday. I wonder, could you confirm that?'

She nodded. 'Or perhaps I should say that I thought

we had a lunch appointment. Bob obviously thought differently, seeing as he stood me up.' She shrugged. 'He's left me hanging around on my own at parties and restaurants often enough in the past because he won't stand up to his bosses, so I suppose I half-expected it. Anyway, I issued the latest in a long line of ultimatums and told him that this time, if he did it again, it would be the last.'

'And was your hus— estranged husband aware that this time you meant it?'

She hesitated. Perhaps she still felt something for the fresh-faced boy she had married, even if he was now flabby, anxious, middle aged and bedevilled by ulcers, because she smiled faintly and gazed at the wedding photo as if reminiscing and said, 'I really don't know. I'd told him the same thing so often, you see. How could he know that this time I meant it?'

It was as neat and evasive an answer as Rafferty had ever heard. And it told them precisely nothing. Somehow, Rafferty doubted she would reveal anything more.

'I think we should have another chat with Harris himself before we see Gallagher,' Rafferty said when they were back in the car. 'I get the feeling Harris won't be quite so discreet on his own behalf.'

Nor was he. They found him at home. Harris was in his pyjamas and he told them he was on sick leave; the sick leave he hadn't dared take before Barstaple's death, Rafferty thought to himself. He couldn't help but wonder if it was significant.

Bob Harris lived in a bedsit just round the corner from the marital home and Rafferty concluded that he either couldn't afford something better than the cheap rented accommodation or had put off buying anything else because hope and uncertainty stopped him; hope that he would get back with his wife and uncertainty that he would succeed in clinging to his job for much longer.

Rafferty remembered he'd meant to ask Harris why Barstaple had called him in to his office for a chat on the day of his murder. And before he asked anything else, he questioned him about it.

Harris seemed to shrivel at the question. Of course this didn't necessarily indicate guilt, Rafferty knew. How could Harris not react suspiciously when Amy Glossop had gone out of her way to make Harris and everyone else aware that, of them all, he had a very good reason for wanting Barstaple dead?

'Mr Harris?' Llewellyn prompted, when Harris failed to respond.

Slowly, Harris looked up. 'What did he want to talk about?' he repeated. Slowly, he shook his head. 'What he always wanted to talk about, of course. The same old things; my inadequacy, my lack of team spirit, my poor grasp of new office technology.'

He shrugged wearily. 'It was his usual technique for getting rid of the older members of staff and it was very effective. I suppose you could say that I knew my days at Aimhurst's were numbered. I'd already listened to the same monologue twice before; this was my third, my final warning. I'm surprised he didn't make sure the letter was written and posted that afternoon. But it's all on my file,' he added. 'Mr Barstaple was always scrupulous about covering his tracks. I had to sign yet another file note agreeing that I was useless.'

Rafferty had read it and an embarrassed silence fell after Harris's pathetic admission. Rafferty felt desperately sorry for him and, aware that more humiliation was in store, was reluctant to resume the questioning.

Although not lacking compassion, Llewellyn was made of sterner stuff and it was he who broke the silence. 'We went to see your estranged wife earlier, sir,' he told Harris. 'She seemed adamant that your separation will now become permanent. You realized this was how she felt?'

Harris didn't even attempt to deny it. He freely admitted that he'd been aware his wife had been determined to make a stand this time. He raised mournful spaniel eyes to Llewellyn's face. 'She's become so much harder in the last year or so. Always before, when she issued ultimatums, she softened them with a smile or a joke.' His voice cracked as he told them, 'This time she didn't.'

'And how did you feel about that?'

'How did I feel?' For the first time during the interview Bob Harris seemed jerked into a semblance of passion. 'How do you think I felt? I felt sick. I still do.' He stared intently at Llewellyn. 'I love my wife very much, Sergeant. I don't want to lose her.' As if the realization that she was already lost to him had hit him anew, Harris's voice flattened. 'But you see she either couldn't or wouldn't understand that the employment market has become a lot tougher, especially for men of my age. She would never accept that I had no choice but to put in long hours when the job demanded it.'

His hand sketched a despairing gesture. 'Oh, I know I'm weak and let people walk all over me, but, with Barstaple, what choice did I have? If I'd stood up to him, I'd have lost my job for certain. And if I'd been rash enough to tell him what I thought of him he would've made sure I could never get another job.' He met Rafferty's eyes. 'I wasn't so desperate, Inspector, that I'd risk that. It's a mistake to lose control, especially with someone like Clive Barstaple. There's always the risk that you'll go too far.'

157

Rafferty nodded. He could imagine that Bob Harris would have a lot more than ulcers burning away in his gut. And when the worm turns . . .

Next on the list was Hal Gallagher. And not before time, thought Rafferty. The trouble was, of course, that they had so many angles to cover they had somehow managed to get sidetracked off the main drag of the investigation. It wouldn't have been so bad had not all of the side alleys so far turned up little or nothing. Their failure rate on the case was one hundred per cent. It didn't help either that Llewellyn seemed obsessed with chasing after even more nebulous elements . . .

Rafferty sighed, only too aware that they should have spent more time on the staff at Aimhurst's than they had so far managed. He was surprised Bradley hadn't yet bawled him out over his handling of the investigation. If only he wasn't so preoccupied with the iffy suit and the trouble it was causing him, he might have his mind more on the job.

Hal Gallagher had a small flat just round the corner from the train station. Its location brought Ross Arnold to Rafferty's mind. Arnold's alibi had checked out; not that Rafferty had really considered him a serious suspect. But the memory of the man made Rafferty wonder, after what Amy Glossop had told them about his argument with Barstaple, whether Gallagher, too, had selected a home in such a location for the purposes of speedy relocation.

Bluff King Hal, as Rafferty had come to think of him, had just finished his evening meal when they arrived. He seemed to live a sparse, bachelor existence, and his home seemed to contain few softening touches such as a woman would bring. Of course, Gallagher had lost his wife, so had perhaps put away pictures or ornaments in order to reduce the painful memories.

Even so, given what Gallagher had said about missing his wife, Rafferty was surprised that, unlike Eileen Harris, he chose not to display his wedding photographs. He concluded that Gallagher must simply prefer to keep his memories in his head rather than displayed on his furniture.

'You've been very frank with us up to press, Mr Gallagher,' Rafferty began, after Hal Gallagher had settled them in his living room. 'So why didn't you choose to tell us that you had had a row with Clive Barstaple on the Friday before his murder?'

Gallagher didn't seem overly worried by Rafferty's abrupt question. He grinned, perched himself on the edge of his dining table, and asked, with every appearance of amusement, 'Why do you think? You got this titbit from Amy Glossop, right? Just my luck that it had to be her who caught me arguing with him. I deliberately waited till everyone had gone to have it out with him.'

Rafferty and Llewellyn exchanged glances. So, they said, it seems as if our engaging American is ready to be as frank as ever.

This cautioned Rafferty to be wary. Such apparent openness was a perfect way to conceal things of a more damaging nature, he knew.

'Have what out with him, exactly?' he asked.

Gallagher raised bushy eyebrows. 'I thought you knew. Hey, are you guys getting me to incriminate myself?'

'Nothing of the kind, Mr Gallagher,' Llewellyn soothed. 'We'd just like to hear your version.'

Gallagher shrugged. 'It's simple enough. I wanted him to ease off Bob Harris. Poor guy was about at the end of his tether. I was scared he might do something desperate.'

It was Rafferty's turn to raise his eyebrows. 'Like murder Barstaple, for instance?' Rafferty was beginning to think that the entire office was trying to pin the murder on Harris. But it seemed he was wrong, because Gallagher immediately contradicted him.

'No. Bob's not the type for that. I was scared he might damage himself, not someone else. I assumed even Clive wouldn't like to have that on his conscience.' He pulled a face. 'Seems I was wrong, though. He didn't give a damn. Was real hard-nosed about it. Had the poor bastard in his office again Wednesday and gave him another roasting. The bottom line with Clive was always the profit margin, the next dollar.' Gallagher gave Rafferty a twisted smile. 'You get the picture?'

Rafferty nodded and smiled. 'I certainly do. You're a real Rembrandt.'

'Not me. Clive was the artist. You've gotta hand it to the guy, he was a master at what he did. He painted most of us into one hell of a corner.' He shrugged. 'Seems one of us decided to break out, that's all, and a piece of trash died. Too bad.'

'And what about you, Mr Gallagher? Did he paint you into a corner, too? It seems pretty clear that most of the staff had good reason to wish Barstaple out of the way. Did you?'

'Me? No, not me. I'm just a dumb guy, but I was smart enough to play Clive's game. That's why I'm still on the payroll. Funny really, I'm the only one who didn't need the job.'

'Oh?'

'Yeah. I did a few deals when I was younger and was able to stash a few dollars away. But a man's gotta have something to occupy him.'

Rafferty wondered by what means Gallagher had

160

managed to 'stash a few dollars' and how large was the
stash. He reminded himself to get Llewellyn to make a few
enquiries about it. He was curious, too, about Gallagher's
relationship with the late Robert Aimhurst, and he asked,
'How did you and Robert Aimhurst meet? I admit, I
thought it strange that you, an American, should work
in such a small British firm. Hardly your style, I would
have thought.'

'I was bumming around the Continent at the time,
France, Italy, places like that, and met Robert Aimhurst
there. He was doing some kind of grand tour and his car
had broken down. I fixed it for him. I've always been
handy that way.' He paused. 'I guess he took a kinda shine
to me. Told me to look him up if I was ever in this neck of
the woods. Well, I was down on my luck – this was before
I made my pile – so I did. That would be back in '67, or
thereabouts. Anyway, I've been here ever since. At first,
I used to chauffeur him around in that fancy Roller of his
and then I guess I graduated to other jobs.' He grinned.
'As Robert Aimhurst's son, Gareth, was more interested
in spending the firm's money than in earning it, I ended
up running the office.' His grin abruptly faded. 'Till the
takeover, anyway.'

Rafferty nodded. He had decided to keep up his sleeve
the fact that Amy Glossop had told them exactly what
Barstaple had said – that he knew something about
Gallagher that the American didn't want to get out.
Time enough to face him with it if, when once he'd
finally got around to contacting them, the FBI came back
to him with something definite.

As he and Llewellyn made their goodbyes and walked
out to the car, he remarked reluctantly, 'I want Hal
Gallagher checked out. I should have done it before,
I know, but what with one thing and another . . .' He

trailed off before he found himself confiding the iffy suit problem to Llewellyn.

When he spoke again, his voice was firmer. 'That story of his about bumming round the Continent struck a false note. He doesn't seem the type for doing such a thing. And as for that chauffeuring job, even when he was younger, I'd have thought Gallagher would have had enough get-up-and-go to fix himself up with something more challenging. Makes you wonder why he didn't.'

He cocked an eyebrow at the Welshman as the lights of the police station appeared ahead of them. 'Maybe there was some reason he didn't want to return to the States. Perhaps he got into some kind of trouble over there that made it too hot for him to return and he charmed old man Aimhurst into giving him a job. From that it wouldn't be too difficult to talk himself into an office job. It's not as if Robert Aimhurst's son sounds like management material. It might be worth investigating if Gallagher had a criminal record in the States.'

Rafferty paused, then went on brightly, in an attempt to take his mind off other aspects of Llewellyn's wedding. 'You know, we haven't sorted out where we're going on your stag night yet. Got any ideas?'

'I have no intention of having a stag night,' Llewellyn told him firmly. 'I know what goes on at these events. They always seem to end with the poor bridegroom tied naked to a lamppost with a bright ribbon tied to a certain part of his anatomy.'

'Not always. Anyway, I'll be there—'

Llewellyn blinked. 'Is that meant to reassure me? Anyway,' he went on, 'if we fail to bring this case to a conclusion in time, Maureen and I may have to postpone the wedding.'

For one blissful moment, Rafferty felt a surge of hope.

That could be the answer to his prayers. Maybe all he needed was more time to come up with a workable scheme to get rid of the suit.

Unfortunately, the surging hope died a quick death as blunt reality hit it over the head. Any delay was unlikely to be for more than a few weeks; and the way his mind was struggling with the iffy suit problem, two years would be insufficient for him to come up with a solution. And if the wedding was delayed, Ma would be sure to blame him for not solving the murder in time. Delay would give him more problems, not less, he realized.

Rafferty bit back another sigh and checked his watch as Llewellyn went through the pernickety toing and froing he called his parking manoeuvres. 'Well, if you're not going to let me get drunk at your expense, I'll be glad if you'd at least let me get out of the car. I'd like to get home before daybreak.'

Llewellyn braked as requested and Rafferty got out. He stuck his head back in the open door and said, 'And if you ever get this car and the white lines aligned to your satisfaction, once you've got that request for information off to the States, you can call it a day as well.'

He slammed the door and decided to leave the latest reports till the next morning. He didn't feel up to them now. What he was looking forward to was a long hot soak in an attempt to get the aches out of his bones. He hoped, too, that a large hot toddy would provide his throbbing head with the wit to come up with answers to all his current problems. He wasn't optimistic. He had more chance of changing Llewellyn's mind about a stag do.

As it happened, he wasn't destined to enjoy either hot bath or hot toddy. He'd just closed his front door behind him and was loosening his tie preparatory to enjoying both when the phone rang. Now what? he thought, as reluctantly he answered it.

Five minutes later, shocked, he replaced the receiver. Then immediately snatched it up again and dialled the station. As he had expected, Llewellyn was still there.

'Dafyd? I've just had Gerry Nunn on the phone.' Gerry Nunn was a sergeant on the uniformed side. 'Amy Glossop's dead. Murdered, Gerry reckons. We'd better get round there.'

Thirteen

'I warned her to be careful,' Rafferty bit out. As he stood outside Amy Glossop's tiny lavatory and stared down at her body, he was eaten up by the guilty conviction that his warning could have been – should have been – more forceful.

Even to his own ears he sounded defensive. Although nobody had accused him of anything, they didn't need to; his overworked, lapsed Catholic conscience provided recrimination enough. Perhaps, if he'd liked Amy Glossop better, he'd have taken more trouble to make her see that secrets could be dangerous.

But he hadn't liked her. And although part of him had pitied her, it hadn't been enough. And now she was dead. Her death a carbon copy of Clive Barstaple's in its ugliness and degradation. And whatever secrets she had were now out of his reach for ever. He supposed it served him right.

He withdrew into the hall, not entirely sure whether the movement was prompted by the overpowering stink of vomit and worse in the enclosed space, or whether, subconsciously, by putting a distance between himself and the corpse, he hoped he would also be able to distance himself from the guilt.

It didn't work, of course. Because this was one death he might have prevented; one death he could have prevented

165

if only he'd taken the trouble. The thought was as bitter as wormwood. Heavy-footed, he walked into the living room. Gerry Nunn followed him.

'You said a worried work colleague of the dead woman rang the station?' Rafferty questioned when he had his emotions and his nausea both under some semblance of control.

Nunn nodded. 'She tried to contact Ms Glossop earlier apparently, but her phone was permanently engaged – off the hook, the operator confirmed. Such behaviour was out of character and her workmate decided to investigate further.'

Rafferty interrupted. 'What's the name of this workmate?'

Gerry Nunn riffled through his notebook. 'A Mrs Steadman. Mrs Marian Steadman.'

Rafferty nodded. Marian Steadman was the sort of woman to concern herself with life's waifs and strays even when the waif was as unpopular as Amy Glossop. Briefly, he wondered why she hadn't mentioned her concern when he'd seen her earlier. But it didn't take much figuring out. Marian Steadman had already made it clear that Amy Glossop must have known her chances of continuing employment at Aimhurst were slim. Maybe she'd concluded that Amy had murdered Barstaple and had done a bunk. Knowing Marian Steadman, she'd have thought Amy Glossop deserved a chance to get away before the hounds were set on her.

'Mrs Steadman came round half an hour ago,' Nunn continued, 'and found the milk still on the doorstep. She knocked, but could get no reply. She looked through the letterbox and Ms Glossop's usual coat was hanging in the hall. The neighbours could tell her nothing. That's when she called the station. We sent a couple of our uniformed blokes round and they broke in. You saw what they found.'

Rafferty nodded again. He remembered that Marian Steadman had been the only one of Aimhurst's staff to make any attempt to understand why Amy Glossop had behaved as she did. Certainly, no one else had a good word to say for her, himself included. Now it seemed likely that she had been killed by one of her colleagues.

But, as he recalled the bleak future that had undoubtedly awaited her, he couldn't entirely discount the possibility that she had killed herself. If she had discovered that Barstaple had deceived her about her job security and that she would have to have her awful mother back home to live with her, it might be enough to drive her to take her own life. Now he asked, 'What do you think to the possibility it was suicide?'

Gerry Nunn shook his head. 'No way. For one thing there was no note. I know that means nothing,' he added, 'but I can't believe anyone in their right mind would choose to die like that. Would you?'

Rafferty shook his head. 'Not me. Far too squeamish. I'd want something painless to see me off.' Gerry was right, he acknowledged. No one in their right mind would choose to die in such an appalling manner. And whatever Barstaple's and Amy Glossop's individual faults, no one had cast doubt on their sanity. If Amy Glossop felt she had reason to kill herself she'd surely have chosen a gentler method.

Sensing someone behind him, Rafferty turned. Llewellyn had arrived and Sam Dally was hard on his heels.

Sam didn't take long to reveal his conclusions; they were the same as Rafferty's. 'I hate to say it, but this death reminds me too strongly of the Barstaple murder for it not to have the same cause – though I'll thank you not to quote me on that till I've done the post-mortem,' he told Rafferty.

Rafferty realized with a shock of horror that they had started back at one again on the corpse tally. He stifled a groan and muttered under his breath, 'Hope this tally doesn't climb to three, too.' Louder, he said again, 'I warned her,' as if he hoped the repetition would help purge his guilt. He appealed to Llewellyn. 'You heard me. You heard me warn her to tell us if she knew anything more.'

Llewellyn's serious brown eyes stared pityingly at him for a few moments, then he said, 'You're convinced she was murdered, then?'

'I reckon so. Don't you?'

Llewellyn raised his shoulders and let them drop before repeating the murder and suicide possibility that Rafferty had already considered and rejected.

Rafferty shook his head. 'I don't buy it for two reasons. One, why would she choose this method of killing herself? Especially when she was aware of what carbohydrate andromedotoxin does to the human body. If what you say was true, she'd have already discovered that she and Barstaple weren't the soul mates she had thought, so would hardly seek to share his pain in death. And two – I can't believe she would be able to hide her guilt over something like murder. You met her. Amy Glossop's face was too revealing of her feelings for her to be able to hide something like that.'

Llewellyn still didn't appear wholly convinced that Amy Glossop had been murdered, but he dropped the subject. 'It's a pity we haven't been able to find that report Barstaple was working on. It would help if we could confirm who was in line for rationalization.'

'I don't think we need the report to figure that one out, do you? The whole lot of them, apart from the Luscious Linda, would have been for the high jump. Stands to reason.'

Still, Rafferty would have liked sight of the report just to confirm it. The rationalization report wasn't in Barstaple's home, it wasn't in his office. It seemed to have vanished along with his lap-top. If Barstaple had been working on it on his lap-top in his office on the evening he died, the only people who would have had the opportunity to take the computer and any print-out would have been Ada Collins, Eric Penn, Mrs Chakraburty or Albert Smith. Yet why would any of them bother? None of them had any reason to fear the rationalization report or its contents.

Rafferty rubbed his throbbing forehead. None of it made sense. If only he could think straight. But his mind just seemed to bounce around between its assortment of worries and guilty feelings – the iffy suit . . . Bradley . . . Amy Glossop.

He sighed and took several calming breaths in an attempt to slow the whirligig of thoughts. Snatching one of them at random, he said, 'I'll need to speak to Marian Steadman. Where is she?'

'I let her go home,' Nunn told him. 'But she said she'd be there the rest of the evening. You've got her address?'

Rafferty started to nod and then realized he hadn't. He'd never been to her home. He realized also that he had got too used to relying on Llewellyn's efficient paperwork to have troubled his head with such details.

Fortunately, Llewellyn broke in and saved him the trouble of admitting it. 'She doesn't live far. We might as well leave the car here, sir.'

Rafferty nodded agreement and they set off, leaving Gerry Nunn and the just-arrived scenes of crime team to deal with the grisly aftermath of death. Rafferty lagged one careful half-step behind Llewellyn all the way to Marian

Steadman's home, so the Welshman would unknowingly guide him. Leading from behind, he believed it was called. Maybe Clive Barstaple should have tried it.

Understandably, Marian Steadman looked pale and shaky, but she managed a brief smile of welcome and led them into a living room attractively decorated in warm rusts and yellows. As they settled on the plumply cushioned sofas, she shook her head. 'Poor Amy. An unhappy life and a miserable death. Strange how some people seem peculiarly cursed by the fates.'

Rafferty nodded sympathetically. He was beginning to feel he and Amy Glossop had been similarly cursed. 'I gather you and the constable found her around seven thirty this evening?'

She confirmed it. 'If only I'd gone sooner.'

Sensitive to 'if onlys', Rafferty was quick to reassure her. 'It wouldn't have made any difference if you had. I'd say she'd been dead some time. Maybe as much as twenty-four hours.'

She could tell them little more. She didn't attempt to find words to describe what she had found after the constables had broken into Amy Glossop's flat. Rafferty was grateful for that. The last thing he needed was a description of the indescribable.

Deciding to leave any report writing till the next morning, Rafferty called it a day. The thought of the hot toddy no longer offered the comfort it had. Because between it and himself stood the bulk of Amy Glossop's mother and the duty of breaking the news of her daughter's death.

The Saturday morning sun was making fitful attempts to break through the clouds. It soon gave up.

Shortly after, fat raindrops began pelting the office

170

windows in earnest. Rafferty, like Llewellyn, in the office early, watched gloomily as they hammered the glass. Rafferty, in an attempt to combat his increasing depression, had put on a bright, pillarbox red tie that morning. But the only effect it had was to cause Llewellyn to blink and screw up his eyes as if they hurt every time he looked at him.

Rafferty was beginning to think he was dragging a permanent raincloud around with him. He hoped it wasn't symbolic, but he couldn't forget that they seemed to be making no inroads into the case at all. Even worse, they now had a second murder to solve.

Sam Dally had been on the phone early, after he'd performed the post-mortem on Amy Glossop. He had confirmed that she had died from the same poison that had killed Clive Barstaple. Rafferty's guess as to the time of her death hadn't been far out according to Sam's findings. He'd said she had been dead between eighteen and twenty-four hours. All he'd found in her stomach – apart from the poison – was coffee.

Lilley and Mary Carmody had already been sent out to check possible alibis. Rafferty wasn't hopeful. Given the time carbohydrate andromedotoxin took to work, he knew she could have been poisoned under their very noses the day after the murder, while they had been at Aimhurst's offices questioning the staff. As Llewellyn would say – it was an ignominious thought.

Another possibility was that she had been killed at home by one of her colleagues, visiting under the guise of friendship.

It was a shame Sam couldn't get the time of death a bit narrower, he thought. Eighteen to twenty-four hours gave the killer plenty of slack.

'Amy Glossop's colleagues were all waiting in that

171

staff room for our arrival on the morning after Barstaple's death,' Rafferty observed. 'I imagine they all had several drinks from that machine. Any one of them could have dropped the poison in her cup. Maybe WPC Green or Smales noticed something. Get them in here, will you, Dafyd?'

However, luck wasn't running Rafferty's way. Neither WPC Green nor Smales had noticed anything. If whoever had poisoned Amy Glossop had done the deed while they were all captive in the staff room that Thursday morning, the killer would need nerve and daring – which seemed at least to let Bob Harris out of the running.

Of course, as he'd already worked out, shaky maths or no, it wasn't certain the poison had been administered while she had been at work.

And when Lilley returned a short time later, it became clear that Amy Glossop's one neighbour had also seen nothing. That wasn't surprising, though. All the doors to the flats were in the alleyway and a high wall separated the neighbour from Amy Glossop. It would have been a lucky fluke if she'd noticed a visitor.

The possibilities chased one another round and round Rafferty's brain till he felt dizzy. He hadn't even managed to come up with an answer to the suit problem, never mind that of the two deaths. He wasn't sure he cared much any more. The second death had put his problem in perspective. He supposed he could always get a job on the buildings when Bradley got him chucked off the force. Get himself a pair of builder's-bum trousers and a hod and he'd be away.

Of course, that still left Llewellyn. Somehow, he couldn't see the elegant Welshman at home on a building site. All those dropped aitches would crucify him.

Rafferty didn't reckon he'd be too keen on the builders' bums, either.

I'll come up with something, he promised his conscience. Just you see if I don't. But even if he managed to sort out that little problem he still had two murders to solve and it wasn't as if they'd yet managed to come close to finding a solution to the first one.

They read through the latest reports in silence. Although convinced that the same person had killed both Barstaple and Amy Glossop, Rafferty wasn't taking any chances. He carried on with the investigation into Barstaple's death as if it was a single event and totally unconnected to the second death.

Lilley had managed to eliminate as suspects in Barstaple's murder all the callers mentioned in Aimhurst and Son's visitors' book. He had checked with various members of staff and they all agreed that none of the outside visitors had gone anywhere near either the kitchen or Barstaple's office.

The staff who had left after the takeover had also been cleared. Two had been receiving in-patient care in hospital for nervous conditions during the relevant time and the third had been in Australia on a long-promised visit to see his grandchildren.

That left the staff at Aimhurst's and any ancient enemies of Barstaple's who had coincidentally found themselves on the same payroll. The checking into that was still on-going and would be for some time.

As well as checking out the local animal-rights activists, Rafferty had put Hanks on to checking whether any of the keys to Aimhurst's premises had gone missing.

There were, he had confirmed, four sets of keys to the premises; the set belonging to Clive Barstaple which Rafferty had appropriated, the second set, held by

Gallagher, the third, held by Albert Smith, and the spare set which was kept in Alistair Plumley's safe. None had been lost or gone missing recently. Of course, that didn't mean that someone hadn't managed to borrow a set and get a copy made.

Rafferty was glad to discover that at least the local animal-rights activists seemed to be out of the running. Amazingly, the rights people had actually admitted to sending the threatening letter to Plumley, but as they had been checked out and had no apparent connection with either Watts and Cutley or Aimhurst's the possibility of them gaining access to the premises was slim. Apart from anything else, it seemed their leading lights had been camped outside an animal laboratory in the north of England for the past fortnight under the watchful eye of the Yorkshire Constabulary.

'Thank God for small mercies,' Rafferty commented. 'At least we're now in a position to see the wood for the trees, which is more than I hoped for when I got here this morning. Now, apart from your alphabet hunt through the country's gazetteers for Dot Flowers, and Lilley's continuing search for ancient grudge-holders, we should be able to concentrate our attentions on the main suspects.

'Fortunately, that holds good for both murders, as, from all we've learned about her, it's clear Amy Glossop's life consisted of work, home, and duty visits to her mother, so it seems unlikely she had the opportunity to learn anyone else's guilty secrets.'

Again, Rafferty felt a stab of pity for Amy Glossop. A pity that only increased his feelings of guilt. He'd visited her mother the previous evening. She'd been exactly as Marian Steadman had implied; selfish, demanding, enormous and more concerned about what would happen

to her than about her daughter's ghastly death. He had cut
the visit as short as decency permitted.

Llewellyn raised his head from the final report and
interrupted his unhappy breast-beating. 'I know we're
digging deeper into the backgrounds of Aimhurst's staff,
particularly that of Hal Gallagher and also that of Albert
Smith, but we seem to have ignored Eric Penn entirely.
We haven't spoken to him again since that initial interview
and I think we should question him once more. I agree
that it's unlikely he killed either of them, but,' Llewellyn
added before Rafferty could interrupt, 'he was one of
those with the opportunity to put the poison in Barstaple's
yoghurt as well as switch the pots. He struck me as being
unnaturally excited over this case. Almost as though he
knew something we didn't and was determined to hold
on to it. You noticed the way he hugged himself when we
interviewed him, as though he was hugging a secret?'

Rafferty waved away the last part of Llewellyn's
observation and addressed the earlier one. 'Of course he
was excited,' he retorted. 'You know what a child he is.
This is probably the biggest thing that's ever happened to
him. He must think it's Christmas, Easter and his birthday
all rolled into one. Anyway, why would he murder Amy
Glossop?'

'We don't know for certain that she was murd—'

Rafferty waved an irritable hand as, once again, the
Welshman quibbled over the second death. He was aware
he was letting his private anxieties spill over into the work
area; the thing was, they were connected. That was the
trouble.

The wedding was getting closer with no resolution to
the suit problem in sight. He was becoming more irritated
by Llewellyn's holier-than-thou attitude concerning law
and the lawbreakers. Why couldn't the bloody man be

more flexible? he asked himself for the hundredth time. If he was, I wouldn't still be distracted from the murder investigation by this farcical iffy whistle dilemma. Wouldn't still be following a dithering line between rapidly reducing alternative solutions.

It wasn't as if he, too, didn't believe the law shouldn't apply to everyone. He did. But, even if he was willing to sacrifice himself and Llewellyn on Bradley's altar, he could hardly let his mother be banged up. And if all the 'taken into considerations' were brought into the equation, that was a distinct possibility. Apart from anything else, if the worst came to the worst and Ma did end up doing time, it would be sure to be his fault; everything else was. She'd make sure he never heard the end of it.

Conscious that his own judgement was shot to pieces, Rafferty knew he ought to listen to Llewellyn's. 'You're right,' he now lamely admitted. 'We should question Eric Penn again. Though if he did kill Barstaple, which I doubt, I would have expected even Eric to have sufficient sense not to let us know he hated him.'

'Possibly. Possibly not.'

Rafferty stared at him. 'You think he had something to do with it, don't you?'

Llewellyn shrugged. 'I don't know. But there's something about him that's been niggling me. It's not just that he seemed excited; as you said, that can easily be explained away. It's more than that. You said he was a child in a man's body. It's true. But he reminds me of a child nursing a secret. A very big secret. Of course, it may be nothing to do with Barstaple's murder. But, before we dismiss him as a suspect, we should try to find out what it is.'

Rafferty nodded and checked his watch, surprised to find that it was still only nine thirty. 'Why don't we go and see him now? He lives with his mother. I think she should be present when we question him. Give her a quick bell, will you? Who knows? She may be better equipped than we are to prise Eric's secret out of him.'

Eric Penn's mother was a widow. And, although tiny in body, scarcely more than 4' 11" by Rafferty's reckoning, her mind more than made up for any bodily limitations. She seemed not only strong, but very sensible.

Rafferty imagined that if she hadn't possessed such strength originally, being solely responsible for a backward son would have forced its development.

In response to Rafferty's questions, she had told them that she had cared for Eric alone for ten years, ever since her husband had died. Eric was their only child.

She ushered them into the sparse but spotless living room of the terraced house. There were no ornaments or vases of flowers in the room. No decorative touches of any kind, Rafferty noted. And, as he watched Eric's jerky arm movements as he lay sprawled full length on the floor playing with an extensive collection of toy cars, he realized why. They wouldn't have lasted long.

Eric seemed far too engrossed in his apocalyptic car smashes to notice them. His mother had to touch his shoulder and speak loudly to him before he realized they were there.

'Tidy your cars away, Eric,' his mother told him firmly. 'There's a good boy. These policemen want to speak to you.'

It was clear the interruption had annoyed Eric. He glanced sullenly over his shoulder at them, his lips pulled downwards like a child whose game had been spoilt.

Mrs Penn obviously drew the line at petulance because

she spoke sternly to him. Amazingly, her giant son obeyed her immediately.

Mrs Penn seemed even tinier beside her son's bulk. It was sheer force of personality, combined with Eric's accustomed obedience that gave her the upper hand in their relationship. God knew what would happen, thought Rafferty, if the day ever came when Eric realized his mother had nothing stronger than a sharp tongue and a quietly authoritative manner to keep him in check.

Eric put his cars in a lidded box under the window and sat on the same box rocking and muttering quietly to himself.

Rafferty spoke his name. The rocking and muttering stopped, but Eric wouldn't look at him. 'Eric,' Rafferty said again. 'We want to ask you some more questions about Mr Barstaple's death. Will you help us?'

Eric darted a brief glance at him and quickly away again. The rocking recommenced.

Mrs Penn intervened. 'Eric. If you know anything about it, I want you to tell these gentlemen.' She paused and added in a sharper tone, 'Are you listening to me, Eric?'

He darted an even briefer glance at his mother, then jerked his head up and down several times.

Mrs Penn turned towards them and said quietly, 'He'll answer your questions. Only,' her voice dropped lower, 'please keep them simple. Otherwise you'll get no good out of him. And you'll need to ask him direct questions if you want answers. It's no good expecting him to pick up hints. He's never been able to understand them. I know.'

This last was said with feeling and Rafferty nodded to show he had understood. He already knew that talking to Eric was like talking to a small child. And children took everything adults said at face value. They had no

178

appreciation of nuances or subtleties. Eric Penn would be the same.

He took a deep breath and began, conscious that if Llewellyn was right, what Eric told them might lead to a killer. 'You remember Wednesday evening, Eric? The evening Mr Barstaple died?'

Eric shot him another sullen look. 'Course I do.'

'That's good. Now, Eric, can you tell me what you remember about that evening? Anything at all.'

Mrs Penn interrupted. 'It's no good expecting him to answer general questions like that. I told you, keep it simple. Eric doesn't do descriptions. You'll have to be specific.'

Chastened, Rafferty tried again. He remembered Llewellyn's talk of secrets and asked, 'Did anyone ask you to keep a secret that day, Eric?'

He shook his head vigorously.

'You're sure?'

Eric nodded equally as vigorously.

'What about at other times?' Llewellyn put in. 'Did anyone ask you to keep a secret at any other time?'

Eric paused, then shook his head again.

Realizing that unless someone had actually specified the word 'secret' to Eric, he mightn't think to mention any euphemisms for same, Rafferty tried another tack. 'Did anyone ask you not to speak about something you saw?'

This brought another emphatic shake of the head. Their other questions brought no more informative answers. Rafferty was rapidly coming to the conclusion that Llewellyn had been mistaken. Eric Penn knew nothing at all. Even if he had, he looked so unhappy, cornered, tormented that He doubted he'd have had the heart to continue pressing him. He was inclined to think they'd been wasting their time. Admittedly, his copper's nose was too distracted to be its usually reliable self, so he couldn't feel certain of this. But as Llewellyn's copper's nose was non-existent and the rest of him permanently infected with the germ of logic, his instincts couldn't be relied on either.

Still, Rafferty told himself as Mrs Penn showed them out, he'd done what Llewellyn wanted and questioned Eric again; was it his fault if it had been the futile exercise he'd expected? Apart from requesting Mrs Penn to continue to probe Eric for anything he might know, Rafferty wasn't prepared to waste any more time on him.

If only my nose was its naturally efficient self, he thought, we might be well on the trail of the murderer by now, almost certainly a double murderer. Unfortunately, his nose was as off-colour as the rest of him, its sniffability to a large extent blocked by other little problems . . .

They got back to the office about ten fifteen. Llewellyn, his nose out of joint, retired for consolation to a spare interview room and his daily stint with his gazetteers.

Rafferty was heading for his own office when Sergeant Beard on the desk shouted after him that he had a visitor. A Mr Alistair Plumley. He'd put him in interview room 1.

Rafferty's surprise at the identity of his visitor was soon overtaken by another; that the previously self-confident Plumley should seem strangely ill at ease. It seemed unlikely to be a feeling with which the boss of Watts and Cutley would be familiar. That he should feel it now made Rafferty curious.

'Did you want to see me about anything important, Mr Plumley?' he asked encouragingly as Plumley seemed reluctant to begin.

Plumley immediately lost his unnatural diffidence. 'Only about these.' He pulled an envelope from his inside breast pocket and dropped it on the table between them. 'I think you'll agree they could be important. They arrived in the post.'

'They?'

'I suggest you look at them.'

Plumley's voice was tight, and Rafferty stared at him before he opened the envelope. It contained several photos and he pulled them out. As he did so he realized why Plumley was not quite himself. The man was embarrassed. And no wonder. The first sight of the photographs was enough to make Rafferty's toes curl.

Fourteen

The photographs were of Clive Barstaple and looked as though they had been taken from outside his bedroom window; Rafferty could just detect what looked like a window frame and the edge of a curtain.

Barstaple was dressed up in the bondage gear that Lilley had found, but there was no doubt it was him. His face in the first snap was turned away from the camera, but each succeeding shot showed it turning further towards it as if someone had tapped on the glass to gain his attention. The last shot showed him full face, his expression startled and the beginnings of fear in his eyes.

Rafferty checked the envelope. The postmark was smeared, but he was able to make out that it was a local one. 'There was no message with these?' he asked Plumley.

'None was necessary, was it?' Plumley replied. 'The message seems obvious to me. Someone was threatening to expose his . . . peccadilloes. Obviously Barstaple didn't react in the way the sender expected so, to fulfil their presumed threat, they sent copies to me. Probably hoped I'd get rid of him when I saw what he got up to in his leisure hours.'

'When did you say these photos arrived?'

'I didn't say.'

Rafferty waited.

After a few moments, Plumley admitted, 'They arrived about a month ago.'

'So why didn't you show them to me immediately after Clive Barstaple was killed?'

Plumley shrugged. 'Let's just say I was considering the situation. Anyway, I'm showing them to you now.'

Rafferty suspected Plumley had debated long and hard about the pros and cons of showing them to him at all. He must be aware that if the photographer turned out to have been implicated in Barstaple's murder, there was no way such pictures could be kept secret. There again, Rafferty frowned, it was possible that Plumley wanted to direct his suspicions elsewhere. Maybe he had discovered Barstaple's side deal with Ross Arnold and resented it. Just because Barstaple had claimed during his argument with Hal Gallagher that Plumley was aware of it and had OK'd it didn't make it true. But if Barstaple's claim was true it still might have been the case that the dead man had cheated Plumley of his share and Plumley had found out. Who knew what these oh-so-ethical business types got up to?

It was yet another angle to be considered, Rafferty realized with dismay. He gazed appraisingly at Plumley for a few moments before dropping his gaze back to the photographs.

They had yet to check Plumley out thoroughly. On the face of it he was in the clear. Like Ross Arnold's alibi, Plumley's had stood up to initial scrutiny. But he was a wealthy man and well able to bribe his way out of trouble. Apart from any other considerations, Plumley was one of only three people apart from the victim himself to have keys to Aimhurst's premises. He could have visited the offices at any time, disconnected the alarm system with his own set of keys and poisoned Barstaple's food with nobody any the wiser.

There again, Rafferty reminded himself, he would hardly be likely to know much about Barstaple's personal dietary arrangements; it was unlikely he and Barstaple had discussed the finer points of the F Plan or any other diet. As far as Plumley was concerned the food in the fridge could have belonged to any member of staff.

Besides, he couldn't imagine a man like Alistair Plumley murdering one of his own hirelings just because he might have drawn the short straw in one minor crooked deal.

Now Rafferty commented, 'I hate to say this, but it's possible that whoever sent you these photographs hadn't attempted to blackmail Barstaple at all. Their aim could have been totally different – using you to get rid of Barstaple. Maybe, after they sent you these photos, they tired of waiting for you to break his contract and got rid of him themselves.'

Plumley nodded. 'I have to agree it's a bit of a coincidence that Barstaple should be murdered a mere month after I received them. I can't believe there's no connection.'

Neither could Rafferty.

A few minutes later he escorted Plumley downstairs and made for his office. He spread the photos out on his desk and gazed at them again. As he did so, into his mind came a picture of the display of photos in Aimhurst's staff room. Like these, they were crisp, sharp, professional. He knew Albert Smith, the Guardian Security guard, had taken them. Had he taken these, too?'

Rafferty shook his head. What possible motive could he have? Further digging had made clear that Smith had never been a victim of Barstaple's previous rationalizing.

And, although Smith's shifty denial that he had heard Barstaple shout for help was curious, Rafferty doubted Smith would have had the opportunity to get to know Barstaple well enough to discover such secrets as the photographs revealed. And even if Barstaple had had homosexual leanings, he thought it unlikely that Albert Smith would have been his type.

Rafferty was still brooding over the photos when Llewellyn returned, scrupulous as ever to take no more than his allotted half-hour on his personal obsession with the country's gazetteers.

Rafferty told him about his visitor and handed over the photographs.

After studying them for a few seconds, Llewellyn commented, 'These were taken by someone who knew what they were doing. Shooting through glass is not something a weekend amateur is likely to have mastered. The reflections would have ruined most such attempts.'

Rafferty had forgotten that Llewellyn was something of a camera buff. It certainly moved Albert Smith further into the frame . . . or did it? He'd told Alistair Plumley that an aggrieved member of staff was probably responsible for the photos. But who amongst the staff was likely to have known of the way Barstaple spent his leisure hours? And Smith wasn't even on the staff. Rafferty certainly couldn't see a man like Clive Barstaple exchanging such chit-chat with a lowly security guard. Barstaple would have kept his little hobby quiet. It was hardly the sort of thing he'd want bruited about. Having others in his power was what he enjoyed; he would have taken care that none of his victims got the chance to reverse roles.

No, Rafferty thought, whoever had taken the photos surely knew Barstaple longer than the three months he'd worked at Aimhurst's, and more intimately than a mere underling at work. With which people are you most yourself? he silently questioned. Who did you let your guard down with? Back came the answer – with your family, that was who. He frowned as he remembered their investigations had revealed that not only had Barstaple never married, he had no brothers or sisters either, and both his parents were dead.

He shared his thoughts with Llewellyn and was just about to order a deeper dig into Barstaple's family background when the phone rang and saved him the trouble.

The voice on the other end of the phone was old, quavery, but still retained an authority that sounded innate. After Rafferty had identified himself, the caller continued.

'My name's Alexander Smith. I am, or rather was, a great-uncle to Clive Barstaple.'

Intrigued, Rafferty gestured to Llewellyn to pick up the other phone.

The line crackled and the voice said loudly, 'Hello? Hello? Are you still there? Damn this infernal machine!'

'Yes, sir. I'm still here,' Rafferty reassured him. 'How can I help you?'

The elderly gent gave a dry cough. 'It's more a case of how I can help you, I think, Inspector.' He paused. 'Look, this is a bit delicate. I don't want to discuss it over the telephone. Could you pop down here for a chat, do you think?'

'Pop where, exactly, sir?'

'Oh, didn't I tell you? I'm sorry. I live in Devon. Just past Exeter.' He added the address, said, 'Come for tea,' and put the phone down.

Bemused, Rafferty replaced the receiver. Clive Barstaple's great-uncle had invited him for tea. He smiled grimly. It would involve a drive of four hours or more. He glanced out of the window. And it was raining again.

He sighed. Still, he did want to know more about Barstaple's background and if that was the only way to get it . . .

'God knows what time I'll be back,' he told Llewellyn as he shrugged into his jacket. 'I'll leave you to hold the fort. Just promise me that if anything useful comes in you'll use your initiative and not sit on it till my return?'

To Rafferty's surprise, instead of protesting at the implied slur, Llewellyn agreed, his manner uncharacteristically meek.

However, Rafferty had neither the time nor the inclination to wonder what the Welshman was plotting. His mind was already taken up with the long journey ahead of him and what, if anything, he might find at its end.

The drive down to Exeter to see Clive Barstaple's great-uncle was every bit as unpleasant as Rafferty had suspected. Rain lashed the windscreen, lorries threw spray across it, blinding him and, to add to the pleasures, which included several multi-mile tailbacks, he got a puncture halfway there.

Altogether, his four-hour journey turned out to be nearer five. It was almost 5 p.m., the beginning of the rush hour, when he finally arrived at Alexander Smith's home. He was tired, wet through and far from in the right frame of mind to listen to the ramblings of an old man who liked to sound mysterious.

Rafferty's frustrations only increased when he met Alexander Smith. For the old man refused to tell him what his phone call had been about until he had had a wash and brush up and had sat down to his meal. This was all laid out on the table in front of the fire in the dark and old-fashioned sitting room when he returned downstairs.

Alexander Smith – or someone – had obviously taken a lot of trouble. There were three different kinds of sandwiches, scones with jam and cream and a large chocolate cake to finish. It was a real old-fashioned high tea, the sort Rafferty hadn't sampled in years. And as he settled by the fire and accepted the delicate bone china cup, he began to feel better.

Alexander Smith seemed as old-fashioned as his home and his high tea. Even though Rafferty guessed he must be around eighty years of age, he was a very upright man and more than a little formidable. His bearing as he sat in his hard leather armchair was a parade-ground shout, the creases in his trousers so razor-sharp they could be construed offensive weapons. Rafferty, more than a little bedraggled and with his flu and his clothes both steaming nicely, wouldn't have been surprised to find himself put on a charge. But even if he looked like the lowliest squaddie on the square, the General, as he was beginning to think of him, treated him with an impeccable politeness.

It was only after he had made sure his visitor was comfortable and had everything he wanted, that the old man began to tell him what had made him telephone.

It soon became clear that it wasn't only Smith's bearing that had a military stamp. From what he now told Rafferty, it was clear that the discipline of a military life had also affected other areas. He intended 'doing his duty', no matter how painful it might be.

Presumably, to save himself the embarrassment of unnecessary explanations, the General now pulled a set of photographs out and spread them on the table by

Rafferty's knees. They were a matching set to those that Plumley had received.

'I received these . . . obscene photographs . . . about a month ago, Inspector,' he revealed. 'I guessed then who had sent them to me, and I was going to deal with it myself.' He hesitated. 'But then, when Clive was murdered, I knew I had no choice but to contact you and it must all come out. I'm sorry I delayed it so long. I found it very – difficult to do.'

His upright body, even his trim military moustache, seemed to wilt a little. But although obviously upset, it was clear he wasn't going to let his distress get in the way of his duty. Gripping the curved handle of his cane more firmly, he said, 'I'm a rich man. I have no children or grandchildren of my own to inherit, so naturally, I was going to leave it to my brother's and sister's heirs, their grandsons, Clive, the grandson of my sister, Lily, and Bertie, the grandson of my brother, John.'

Some memory fleetingly stirred in Rafferty's tired brain, but the warmth of the fire and the sluggishness induced by a full stomach made the memory too drowsy to rise to the surface. It faded away as the General continued.

'But then Bertie tried to do his cousin out of his share by accusing him of—' A spasm of pain passed over the old man's face and his knuckles whitened on the cane. It was several seconds before he continued. 'He accused Clive of going in for unnatural practices. He told me he had caught him masturbating, wearing—' He winced, then forced himself on again. 'Wearing women's undergarments, and a scarf belonging to my late sister. Naturally, I didn't believe him. I was so disgusted with him I told him I was cutting him out of my will.'

The General passed a mottled hand over his lined forehead as he glanced again at the display of photographs. 'It seems he was right all along.'

'Excuse me, sir, but how long ago did all this happen?'

'How long? Twelve years ago. When Clive was sixteen and Bertie twenty.'

'Why did you refuse to believe your great-nephew, Bertie, when he told you?'

'Would you want to believe it of one of your family, Inspector?'

Slowly, Rafferty shook his head. 'I suppose not.' It was hard to imagine any of his family going in for such practices; even the women preferred their undergarments warm and comfortable. 'Certainly, I wouldn't unless I had proof.' And even then . . .

'Exactly what I demanded.' Alexander Smith gestured at the photographs. 'It seems Bertie took me at my word. It took him a long time, but he finally managed to produce some.'

The General gazed into the fire, his expression bleak. 'Bertie's wicked behaviour won't benefit him. He's shown himself unworthy to be my heir. As for Clive—' Another spasm crossed his face and was as quickly gone. 'I admit I was fond of the boy. I had, in the past, made excuses for him. His father was an unpleasant man. He treated the boy dreadfully when he was young, punishing him severely for the slightest misdemeanour or even for nothing at all. It turned the boy in on himself. Made him hate. I suppose it made him want to inflict pain back, to punish as he had himself been punished as a child, cruelly and for no reason.'

The General straightened his back. 'But I've made an end to excuses. There are some things I find myself unable

190

to excuse and such perversions are amongst them.' He paused. 'In many ways it's a pity the gal's not a boy. She was always the best of the bunch, mentally far tougher than either of the boys. But there, you can't leave your money to a girl.'

Rafferty was about to say that was a very old-fashioned attitude, then he thought better of it. What other attitude could a man of Alexander Smith's age be expected to exhibit?

But it seemed the old gentleman had guessed Rafferty's thoughts, for his faded eyes twinkled briefly. 'Yes, I'm old-fashioned about such matters. I make no apology for it. Girls are so much at risk from fortune-hunters. At least I knew that Clive and Albert would have been hard-headed enough to hang on to the money once they'd got it. My great-niece has always been prone to listen to hard-luck tales. She gets it from my sister. It makes her vulnerable, for all that she's a sensible enough lass. And, of course, now she's a widow, it makes her doubly vulnerable.

'I firmly believe that it was Albert, my other great-nephew, who sent me these pictures, Inspector, presumably hoping to get himself reinstated in my will. Until Clive started work there they would have had no contact. Hardly surprisingly, they hated one another.'

'Albert?' Rafferty repeated slowly. 'Albert Smith, you mean? The Albert Smith who works as a security guard at the firm where Clive was killed?'

This time the General's mannered demeanour was less than impeccable. The look he gave Rafferty was surely the one he reserved for inferiors who refused to go over the top in battle. 'Yes, of course.' The bite of the parade-ground entered his voice. 'Good God man, who did you think I meant?'

Rafferty excused his slowness. 'It's been a long day.'

191

'Perhaps I should mention that my great-niece, Marian – Marian Steadman – also works there. She's Albert's sister,' he explained.

Rafferty decided his head cold must have penetrated as far as his brain. He really had been incredibly stupid not to have cottoned on to the fact of 'Bertie's' identity before. Now he knew about the relationship, the family likeness was apparent. Both Marian Steadman and Albert Smith had dark hair and dark eyes. Both had very similar looks; even their gestures were the same, he realized as he recalled the disagreement he had observed between them through the glass of Aimhurst's reception area. They were really extraordinarily alike; that was if you discounted Albert's balding scalp, small, greying moustache, and horn-rimmed spectacles.

'Surely, Clive must have recognized his cousin and insisted he was replaced with someone else?'

'Doubt he would recognize him,' the General told him. 'Albert's changed a lot in the intervening years. He's aged considerably. Last time I saw him, he had lost most of his hair, started wearing heavy spectacles, and grown a little military moustache – probably in a failed attempt to ingratiate himself with me. To my knowledge they hadn't set eyes on one another for years, not since Clive was a boy. Besides, I imagine, to protect her brother's job, Marian would soon head him off if he showed the slightest sign of recognizing him. It would have helped, too, that Smith's such a common name.'

'You didn't mention the matter to Clive?'

'No. Marian asked me not to. Said it was better that way as Clive obviously didn't recognize his cousin.'

The double blow of one great-nephew's murder and revealed perversity and the other's vindictiveness had obviously taken its toll of Alexander Smith. Not unnaturally, such events would be shocking enough to a younger man, but in a person of Smith's age and rigid code, their combined weight could be enough kill him. However, as Rafferty was about to learn, the General's train of thought had again leapt ahead of his and his next words revealed he had concerns of an even greater magnitude on his mind.

'And now it's come to this.' His voice faltered. 'Maybe it would have been better if I had mentioned it. At least Clive would still be alive and Albert – Albert wouldn't have had the temptation to kill put in his path.'

As the full horror of the General's concerns were made clear, Rafferty felt he had to offer a tentative comfort. 'You can't be sure your other nephew killed Clive, sir.'

'Can't I, Inspector?' Alexander Smith grasped his cane firmly with both hands. As though its solidity strengthened his resolve, his back straightened again. Now he was facing facts squarely and Rafferty could gauge something of the hard officer he must once have been. Hard but fair, he guessed, but nonetheless, certainly not someone to offend in the way Albert Smith had offended him.

The fire drew the General's gaze again and he stared into its heart. 'Who else had the strong motive my elder great-nephew possessed? I gather from the newspapers that Clive was killed in his office, in premises that were secure. Obviously, he was poisoned by someone who knew his routine, someone who had good reason to want to do him harm. He'd only been with that firm for three months. I hardly think that's long enough for him to have made an enemy amongst his colleagues. Certainly not an enemy who could wish him dead. No, Inspector. I think we can safely say it was a long-standing grievance that brought about Clive's death and no one but Albert could have had such a motive or the means to get close enough to poison him.'

Rafferty didn't feel able to tell the General that his favourite great-nephew had grown into as unpleasant a man as his father; had, in fact, been a man more than capable of attracting killing enemies in three weeks, never mind three months.

Instead, he too, gazed into the flames. And as he did so, he saw not only the flames, not only that Smith had had the opportunity to steal both the lap-top and the rationalization report – either for a piece of added mischief or to delay any sackings for his sister's sake – but also that it was probable the General was right after all. For Albert Smith, whom he had largely discounted from the investigation for want of a motive, stood revealed as having the very best of reasons for murder, the oldest in the world. An unholy triumvirate of reasons; greed, jealousy and revenge.

Fifteen

Thankfully, the rush hour had nearly finished by the time Rafferty started the return journey and he made it in less than half the time.

Back at the station, he hurried along to his office, confident that Llewellyn would still be there; probably compiling more lists from his collection of gazetteers. To his surprise, the office was empty, the lights were off and the room had that lonely, desolate air that hangs around places when the inhabitants have long gone.

Puzzled, Rafferty walked along the corridor to the CID room and thrust open the door. 'Anyone seen Sergeant Llewellyn?' he asked of the room at large.

Only Lilley, still working on his own lists, and Hanks, who was helping him, were in occupation. They both shook their heads. More puzzled than ever and starting to get irritated at this latest disappearing act in the case, Rafferty withdrew and made for the canteen.

WPC Green was there. She looked up guiltily as Rafferty appeared in the doorway and abruptly demanded, 'Seen Sergeant Llewellyn?'

Lizzie Green leapt to her feet. 'No, sir. Not for hours.'

'Well, if you do, tell him I want to see him.'

The shutters were down on the serving counter and he had to be content with a cup of weak machine tea. Being unable to immediately share his discoveries in the case with his second-in-command brought a return of his previous irritation. He might have found the answer to one puzzle, but now he had another, lesser one to replace it; where was the bloody man when you wanted him? He surely couldn't have gone home when he'd been left to hold the fort.

He strode back to his office, switching the hot plastic cup from hand to hand and slopping tea as he went. He tried Llewellyn's home number and got no answer. He toyed with the idea of ringing Maureen's mother in case he was there fighting the good fight over the wedding-guest list and decided against it.

At least, he reminded himself, they seemed to be getting to the bottom of the case. And not only that— The phone rang ten seconds after he had replaced the receiver, breaking his train of thought.

Llewellyn, he thought, at last, as he snatched up the receiver. He was just about to launch into a tirade when a voice that was definitely not Llewellyn's began to speak.

It was an American voice, and as strongly Noo Yoik as Hal Gallagher's. Rafferty sat up straight as the voice in his ear introduced himself, then checked he was speaking to the 'main man', as he described Rafferty.

Rafferty blinked at the description, but let it ride. He even managed to agree that he was the main man. When he did so, the detective on the other end said something even more astonishing; that Hal Gallagher had been a suspect in a murder case in the States.

The hairs on the back of Rafferty's neck rose even further as Detective First-class Swaney's voice twanged in his ear with further information.

'It was a poisoning case. The killer used some plant poison I'd never heard of, but the lab said it came from the rhododendron plant of all things. We never caught the killer.'

196

Rafferty recovered sufficiently from the sudden flurry of surprises to ask, 'And Gallagher was a strong suspect?'

He sensed the shrug at the other end. 'No stronger than half a dozen others, but he skipped before we could get a case together. Even though it happened years ago, I remembered the investigation because it happened just after I joined the department.'

Deprived of Llewellyn's listening ear, Rafferty took the opportunity to impress the American. It gave him immense satisfaction to be able to tell him, 'Well, we've found him for you. Of course, he may face charges here first, but if you want to get an extradition together—'

'No point.' Bluntly, Swaney broke into Rafferty's self-congratulations, his manner indicating a determination to squash them. 'The only witness we had totalled himself in an auto smash last year. Even if Gallagher was the murderer, it would never get to court now.' Swaney paused and allowed a hint of curiosity to enter his voice. 'So you reckon our guy might have been the perp in your investigation?'

Familiar as he was with American movies, Rafferty had no trouble understanding the Yank detective's verbal shorthand.

'Could be,' he temporized. 'But, as in your case, Detective, he's one of a number of possible suspects, though what you've told me is certainly interesting. Could you let me have a mugshot of your Gallagher? I want to be absolutely certain it's the same man.'

'Sure thing. I'll get it on the wire to you, like yesterday.'

Swaney broke the connection and Rafferty sat back. No wonder Gallagher had been bumming around the Continent. He couldn't go home. At the time he'd thought

Gallagher made an unlikely backpacker. No wonder, either, that he had latched on to Robert Aimhurst.

Rafferty frowned down at his forgotten tea. It had a skin on it and he thrust it away in disgust. Now he had not one, but two prime suspects. He'd been more than satisfied with the one; but two only added doubts, uncertainties.

Dammit, he muttered again. Where the hell was Llewellyn? He really needed to talk this whole thing through with him. Accused too often of going off bull-headed after a suspect, Rafferty was becoming increasingly sensitive to the charge. He was unwilling to conduct potentially explosive interviews without Llewellyn's restraining presence. And the damn man was nowhere to be found.

He was still sitting there an hour later. Only by then, he was no longer excited or even frustrated at Llewellyn's unexplained absence. He was good and mad. Admittedly, eleven thirty at night was not a good time to begin important interviews. After driving to Devon and back, he felt too tired, anyway. But, contrarily, he decided that wasn't the point. He should have been able to rely on Llewellyn's support if he had decided to interview Smith and Gallagher. It was especially galling as he suspected his frustration at not being able to discuss his latest discoveries would probably have choked him before Llewellyn showed his face again.

Why did the bloody man have to choose now, of all times, to do a disappearing act? It wasn't as if they hadn't had enough of those already.

The station was surprisingly quiet. Even the drunks had stopped shouting when Rafferty's door creaked and he looked up.

Llewellyn was standing in the doorway. 'I saw the light,' he began.

'Hallelujah,' Rafferty muttered. 'Ma'll be pleased.'

'And wondered if you might still be here.'

'Oh, I'm here. I've been here for hours. The question is where the bloody hell have you been?' Tired and sickening with the flu as he was, Rafferty found sufficient energy to work himself into a temper. 'I don't know. I leave you in charge for a few hours and you bugger off to God knows where without a word, when I—'

'I did leave a message, sir. With Smales,' Llewellyn quickly broke in, obviously hoping to end the torrent. It was a singularly unsuccessful hope.

'Smales?' Rafferty's eyes narrowed. 'Didn't want to be found, I take it?'

Constable Smales suffered from a chronic inability to pass on messages which could be quite convenient if a colleague wanted to cover himself.

Llewellyn said nothing, but looked exceedingly pleased with life.

'So what have you been doing?' Rafferty asked tartly. 'Come on, spit it out.'

'I've been using my initiative, sir, as you suggested.'

'Initiative, is it? Don't get cocky with me,' Rafferty warned. 'I'm not in the mood.'

'I've been to Birmingham.'

'What did you want to go there for? I thought we'd already discounted—'

'Chasing a hunch. You didn't seem terribly interested in anyone but those you considered the main suspects and—' Rafferty went to butt in to refute this slur, but honesty compelled him to admit Llewellyn was right and he waved to him to go on. 'But it occurred to me there might have been a genuine reason for Mrs Flowers, the

199

missing cleaner, to have hit on Birmingham when she gave Ada Collins her excuse for missing work.'

Rafferty was about to point out that Llewellyn himself had discovered that there was some doubt whether she had even said Birmingham, but instead he asked, 'And was there?'

Llewellyn nodded. He produced a list and pointed to a name. 'Bit of a coincidence, don't you think, that Anderson, the chap Barstaple sacked, and who died earlier this year, should have been admitted to a Birmingham hospital?'

Rafferty stared at him. 'You think there's a connection between this Michael Anderson and Mrs Flowers?'

'I know there is. And as we have been unable to confirm her identity, I thought we might at least confirm his.'

Llewellyn paused as if to gather his thoughts and Rafferty burst out, 'Well, go on, then. Get on with it, for God's sake.'

'Turns out that Michael Anderson and Mrs Flowers' son were one and the same.'

Rafferty's jaw dropped. Stupidly, he stared at Llewellyn. 'You mean . . . ?' He frowned. 'What do you mean, exactly?'

'Remember Ada Collins mentioned that Mrs Flowers' son had been something of a trial to her?'

Rafferty nodded.

'She also mentioned that he must have a police record. I borrowed one of the photographs of Michael Anderson taken at the post-mortem, plus a set of his fingerprints, and checked the record and mugshot under that name. Turns out his mother was Mrs Dorothy Pearson. Anderson was her maiden name. She had him while she was still unmarried.'

Rafferty's memory, which felt it had covered a period

of weeks instead of days, had to struggle before he made the connection. 'Pearson? But that's the name of the second suicide we found the day of Barstaple's murder. You mean she was actually Dot Flowers?'

'The very same. She called herself Flowers for reasons of her own, nothing to do with concealing her identity from the authorities. At least, not directly.'

'You mean she was never an illegal at all?'

Llewellyn shook his head.

'OK,' said Rafferty. 'So why, exactly, did she use an alias?'

'I wondered about that and went round to see her GP before I came back here. I had to get him out of bed. He told me that after her husband died, she had lived with a man called Flowers for years; but he had always refused to marry her. He only died a few years ago. She kept her own name for official things like her GP's list and for tax and insurance purposes, but adopted the name Flowers for the sake of the neighbours. People of her generation are still sensitive about that sort of thing.'

Slowly, Rafferty nodded. Now he remembered something his ma had said about Her Next Door's daughter. Called herself Mrs Williams, Ma had said, adding that she knew very well she hadn't any right to the name as she wasn't married to Mr Williams.

'Pity her GP didn't think of sharing this information with us before,' Rafferty commented. 'Doesn't he read the papers? We've had Mrs Flowers' name and photofit adorning them all for the last few days.'

'He didn't see them,' Llewellyn told him. 'If you remember, he told us he was just off on a fishing trip. He's only just got back. Said he always makes a point of cutting himself off from civilization. The place he goes to, Gartloch Lodge, is in the Scottish Highlands

201

and makes a special feature of the back to basics bit; no phones, newspapers, television or radio. Nothing but fishing and talking, and drinking.'

Rafferty nodded again. So that explained it. Gartloch Lodge sounded just his kind of place. Perhaps he'd book a holiday there in the spring – if he managed to avoid holidaying at Her Majesty's pleasure, that was.

'We still can't be sure that she killed Clive Barstaple,' Rafferty pointed out. 'And what about Amy Glossop? You're surely not suggesting she somehow killed her as well?'

'Hardly.'

'So who did?'

'No one. Amy Glossop killed herself.'

'But why?'

'The usual reasons, I imagine. Despair, fear of the future, loneliness.'

'But she didn't even know what he'd died of, none of them did. All they were told was that he had been poison—' Rafferty broke off abruptly, his eyes narrowed and he swore. 'Smales – got to be him who let the cat out of the bag. Who else? He was so cock-a-hoop about being right on the type of poison used. He got right up Dally's nose. Bloody idiot. I'll deal with him in the morning.' After this brief outburst, Rafferty paused again, and then said, 'But surely even he wouldn't have been so stupid as to supply the gory details?'

'I don't think he can have done, do you?' Llewellyn replied. 'If she'd known how awful Barstaple's death was she wouldn't have chosen the same method. Obviously, all she knew was the name of the plant. Who would have told her the gory details, as you term it? And when? She went home on Thursday lunchtime after we'd interviewed all the staff and, as far as we're aware, she saw nobody else.

202

The other staff retired to the pub without her and she'd been dead at least eighteen hours by the time Marian Steadman found her. She had no opportunity to learn more about the manner of his death.'

Llewellyn paused for breath before continuing. 'So, yes, I do believe she killed herself using the same means as Barstaple's murderer. She didn't know what it had done to him, didn't know its horrific symptoms. It must have seemed both simple and expedient to use the same poison to commit suicide. Not only would she leave a miserable existence, but she would also put her colleagues under a double load of suspicion. I imagine she found the thought very satisfying. You've said often enough yourself that suicides are frequently amazingly ignorant about the means they choose to end their lives. Few of them seem to take the trouble to discover exactly what their chosen method will do to them.'

Rafferty was silent for several minutes while he digested it all. Then he realized that Llewellyn hadn't answered the first part of his question and now he repeated it. 'OK,' he admitted, 'you've convinced me. But where's your proof that Dot Flowers killed Barstaple?'

Llewellyn produced a small plastic bottle of some pale liquid. 'I found this in Mrs Flowers' rubbish bin. Fortunately, she'd forgotten to put the rubbish out for the refuse disposal people before she killed herself. It was still there, waiting for us to find it.'

Rafferty tried to imagine the immaculate Llewellyn voluntarily plunging his hands into someone else's rubbish and failed. 'So what is it?' he asked, though he had already guessed.

'Carbohydrate andromedotoxin,' Llewellyn replied.

Rafferty was impressed. 'Bloody hell, what did you do to get the results so fast? Threaten to blow the lab up?'

Forensic were not noted for their high speed response times, as Rafferty knew.

'I didn't send all of it to the lab. I asked an old university acquaintance on the staff of a local chemical firm to analyse some of it for me.' Llewellyn quickly defended his unethical approach. 'I felt the need for speed was more important than confidentiality. Anyway, confidentiality isn't a problem. The forensic laboratory is more full of leaks than this chap.'

'Have I complained?' Rafferty asked. 'I'm all for a bit of initiative, me. Especially if it gets this blasted case over and done with.'

His words concealed the fact that Llewellyn had robbed him of his usual glory. Briefly, he put Llewellyn in the picture about his own discoveries. They had gone decidedly flat.

'Ironic, isn't it?' he now asked. 'That Mrs Pearson or Flowers, whatever you want to call her, should care so much what the neighbours thought when the current lot obviously couldn't give a damn if she lived over the brush with ten men. They barely remembered her first name, never mind anything else.'

'She didn't adopt it for their benefit,' Llewellyn told him. 'She adopted it years ago when she and the late Mr Flowers first moved to Elmhurst. Of course, this was at a time when it was a stigma to live in sin. I suppose she felt that once she was known by the name by people in her neighbourhood, she could hardly change it back without drawing attention to her deception.'

Suddenly, the tiredness got to Rafferty. He felt drained. He wanted to go home. Doggedly, he insisted on hearing the rest of it. 'I suppose she blamed Barstaple for her son's death?'

'Undoubtedly. Ever since he sacked him, Michael

Anderson had gone downhill. He couldn't get another decent job, he became depressed, started taking drugs, sleeping rough, getting into trouble with the police. A frequent enough story these days. According to the reports, when he died of an overdose earlier this year it was the first his mother had heard of him for some weeks. It must have been a terrible shock to her.'

Rafferty nodded.

'I imagine her son must have mentioned that Barstaple was working at Aimhurst's. You remember I told you that Michael Anderson had worked there for a short time as a cleaner?'

Rafferty nodded again.

'I suppose she started making her plans then,' Llewellyn continued. 'Got herself taken on by Allways after her son's death.'

'So who swapped the yoghurt containers? No.' Rafferty held up his hand. 'Don't tell me.' He was determined to come up with some answers on the case. 'I think I can guess.' He hoped so, anyway. He needed to feel he'd made some contribution, however small. 'Eric Penn, right?'

Llewellyn nodded. 'That's my belief, though, of course, I have yet to question him. According to Ada Collins, who I have spoken to again, Mrs Flowers had taken him under her wing. She felt sorry for him. He must have been pleased she trusted him to do something for her. He must also have been bursting to tell someone about it. Only I suppose he was scared he'd get into trouble, so he said nothing. I imagine, for his own sake, she had impressed upon him that he had to keep quiet.'

Llewellyn went on to fill in further details of his triumph, but Rafferty was no longer listening; he was nursing his bruised pride.

It was the first time Llewellyn had beaten him to the

solution of a murder investigation. He wasn't sure he liked it. In fact, he was damn sure he didn't.

You'll have to look to your laurels, Rafferty, my boy, he told himself. Instinct was the only thing he'd had over Llewellyn; now it looked as if Llewellyn was developing some instincts of his own.

Of course, he comforted himself, he'd been at a decided disadvantage in solving this murder, weighed down as he'd been – as he still was – with the iffy suit problem. Obviously, it had preoccupied him to such an extent that Llewellyn had been able to surge ahead in solving the case. Not only that, Rafferty now realized; he'd also taken over a large part of the initiative and Rafferty had just gone along with it. Still, it was hardly an omen of things to come, he assured himself. Nothing like it.

Llewellyn broke into his thoughts. 'I'm surprised you didn't get there before me. You always have before.'

Although Llewellyn's tone betrayed the merest touch of that intellectual arrogance that had been much in evidence when they had worked on their first case together, Rafferty was sensitive to it. Indignant, he found himself on the brink of saying that he would have solved it if it hadn't been for that blasted suit. He stopped himself just in time.

Instead, he winked, gave Llewellyn what he fondly imagined was an enigmatic smile, and, after telling his stirring conscience to shut up, said, 'Thought it was time you got there on your own, boyo. Why don't we just call it an early wedding present?'

Although it seemed probable that Llewellyn's conclusions about the case had been correct, with the murderer herself dead before her victim they could never prove it conclusively. But, for his own satisfaction, Rafferty wanted to tie up the loose ends. He did so the next day.

Gallagher admitted he had been a suspect in the sixties murder, but insisted he had been framed. Rafferty was inclined to believe him. He even told him he could probably return to the States now as it was unlikely the police would reopen the case.

After being put in the picture, Eric Penn's mother got the truth from her son with little difficulty. As Llewellyn and Rafferty had guessed, Eric had swapped the containers in Barstaple's litter bin, first flushing the second container's contents down the sink. He'd done it because Dot Flowers had always been kind to him and it had made him feel important to be asked.

Rafferty also spoke to Albert Smith and Marian Steadman. He didn't want Smith to think he'd got away entirely with his wicked behaviour.

He found them both in Marian Steadman's home. After she had let him in he followed her into the comfortable living room where he'd dropped the twin packets of *in flagrante delicto* photos of Clive Barstaple on the coffee table, upending first one, then the other.

As the shots of Clive Barstaple in his bondage gear cascaded on to the wooden table Marian Steadman gasped and her face drained of colour. Her gaze flashed quickly towards her brother, then away again. Steadily, she met Rafferty's eyes. 'I don't understand. Why are you showing us these?'

'Because whoever took them sent one lot to Alistair Plumley and the other to Alexander Smith, your great-uncle, as well as Clive Barstaple's. Bit of a coincidence that he should receive the same explicit, compromising pictures, don't you think?'

She said nothing.

'Mr Smith senior phoned me soon after he heard of Barstaple's murder. I went down to Devon to see him.'

207

Rafferty gestured down at the lurid shots of Barstaple. 'He had a good idea who had sent them, you see.' He glanced at Albert Smith's rigid back. 'I think he was right.'

Marian Steadman turned to her brother. 'Bertie? Is this true? Tell me.'

Albert Smith turned slowly at his sister's anguished voice as if reluctant to face her. 'I don't know what he's talking about. Why would I take such pictures?'

'That's an easy one,' said Rafferty. 'To discredit your cousin in your uncle's eyes. To do likewise in Plumley's.'

Smith was, it seemed, determined to keep up the pretence right to the bitter end. 'What would be the point?' he demanded. 'I'm not even in the old man's will.'

'No, but you were hoping to be, weren't you? Once you'd brought your cousin's little peccadilloes to his attention you were sure you would shine by comparison.'

Smith glowered at him, but stayed silent.

His sister had a rather more sensible approach than sulks. 'It's no good, Bertie. Can't you see you're doing yourself – and me – more harm than good?'

With ill grace, Albert Smith conceded that she was right. He smoothed his thinning dark hair self-consciously over his bald patch and faced Rafferty. 'All right,' he admitted, 'I did hope the old boy would put me back in his will. Why not? And he had a right to know the truth about Clive.'

He had the right to know the whole truth about both his great-nephews, thought Rafferty, but he hoped he never did. He felt sorry for the straight-as-a-die old man. How had bloodlines that had produced a man like the General spawned such descendants as Barstaple and Smith?

Marian Steadman turned to Rafferty. 'I want you to be clear on one thing, Inspector, that whatever else Bertie did, he didn't kill Clive.'

208

'That's right,' Smith chimed in. 'And you'll never prove otherwise. All I wanted to do was to remove him from his post and from my great-uncle's will, nothing more. I swear I intended nothing more.'

You would say that, wouldn't you, thought Rafferty, as the words of another time, another place, another scandal came into his mind. He hadn't yet explained that they already knew the name of the killer. Dorothy Flowers/Pearson was safe in the next world and unlikely to reveal the truth of the matter. He was tempted to let this explanation wait. Then he glanced at Marian Steadman's anguished expression and knew she didn't deserve such treatment.

'You weren't technically guilty of his death,' he admitted to Smith, 'although some would disagree. But no one would argue that morally you don't bear a heavy responsibility. It was a nice little bonus, wasn't it, to have him out of the running for ever? You're surely not still trying to pretend you didn't hear his shouts for help?'

Although he admitted nothing, Smith had the grace to flush and lower his eyes.

'If you'd answered his cries you might have saved his life. But you didn't want that, did you? You wanted him dead. Only you didn't have the guts to do it yourself.'

Pale before, now Smith went the colour of tallow. He wouldn't meet either of their eyes, even when his sister said pleadingly, 'Bertie? Did you . . . ?' And received her answer in his silence.

'There was one other thing you could help us with, Mr Smith,' Rafferty told him. 'If you would be so kind. It was you who took Barstaple's lap-top and rationalization report, wasn't it?'

Smith's mouth tightened. And when he made no reply, his sister spoke for him. 'Yes, he did. That much he did tell me.' Her voice lowered as if to plead with Rafferty to understand. 'Clive was already dead and Bertie saw the report on the desk and took it, along with the computer. He did it for me. Thought it would help me. Though how . . .' Her gaze flickered hopelessly over to her brother and then back to Rafferty. 'He thought he was helping me,' she insisted.

Rafferty nodded, giving Smith the benefit of the doubt over that at least.

All at once, Rafferty tired of the man, of his deliberate deafness, his cowardice, the way he tried to hide behind his sister's skirts.

'Don't make any travel plans, Mr Smith,' he warned as he turned on his heel and made for the door. 'We may wish to charge you with other offences; like attempted blackmail and obstruction. Like sending obscene materials through the post.' Not to mention lack of common humanity, he added silently as he let himself out.

Epilogue

L lewellyn and Maureen's wedding day dawned clear, bright and sunny; a perfect spring day in fact, which, considering it was still only March, was a miracle. Doubly so, as not only autumn, but winter, too, had borne more than a passing resemblance to India's monsoon season.

Wryly, Rafferty shook his head as he pulled up outside the groom's flat and adjusted the buttonhole in his hastily purchased new suit. Whoever had said that the sun shone on the righteous hadn't got it quite right, he thought. Now, if he'd said the sun shone on the self-righteous he'd have hit the bull dead centre.

He walked up Llewellyn's path and gave a fancy rat-tat-tat on his front door. When Llewellyn answered, Rafferty was surprised to see that his sergeant's face was a beautiful pea-green – thinking about his soon-to-be mother-in-law, Rafferty surmised. The pea-green colouring didn't go with his elegant dove-grey wedding suit at all. But Rafferty had a remedy for that. He chivvied the bridegroom back inside and shut the door.

'What you want is a good strong coffee,' he decided, then paused, head on one side, hand reaching inside his jacket. 'Unless I can tempt you to something more effective?'

Llewellyn shook his head.

'Come on, then. Let's get something other than bile into

211

your stomach. Can't have you ruining the photographs. Have you eaten?'

'No. My stomach's too upset. I don't think I'll keep anything down.'

'Consider yourself lucky you're only likely to get married once then.' Rafferty wished post-mortems came round as infrequently. His stomach would be far happier, if so. He studied the bridegroom and prescribed some dry toast, holding up an admonishing finger as Llewellyn began to argue. 'And before you start, remember I'm your best man and today there's no doubt that I'm in charge. For once, you'll do what you're told and like it.'

The toast and coffee were soon prepared and Rafferty carried them into Llewellyn's elegant minimalist living room. 'Get that down you,' he ordered and watched as Llewellyn did what he was told.

While Llewellyn ate, Rafferty eyed him and the wedding suit speculatively. He had nearly managed to convince himself that if he could get through today without Superintendent Bradley finding out anything about the suit both their jobs would be safe. After all, he had more or less persuaded himself, Llewellyn would hardly wear such a quality suit for work.

This reassuring thought was immediately followed by another. Yes, he would. He's not like you, Rafferty, with your Sunday best outfits that only get worn at weddings and funerals. Llewellyn liked to look like a bobby-dazzler every day. Leaving his best gear in the wardrobe for the greater part of the year wasn't his style at all.

OK, Rafferty thought, so the iffy whistle was going to be given regular airings; he'd deal with that problem later. Meanwhile – as he forced himself to face the fact that not recognizing a very sharp suit when he saw one wasn't Bradley's style – he knew he had the here and now of today to sort out.

With the toast and coffee inside him, Llewellyn's pea-green colour faded. And, although he still seemed as tight as an overwound watch, it somehow suited him. The drawn features looked as sharp as the iffy suit and Rafferty felt a twinge of regret.

But he had no choice. Like Alexander Smith, he knew his duty and would do it, come what may. He couldn't understand why it had taken him so long to come to such an obvious solution to his dilemma.

Briefly, Rafferty closed his eyes, then, pausing only to send a prayer for forgiveness up to St Michael, he staged a deliberate stumble over one of Llewellyn's expensive-looking rugs and managed to throw the entire contents of his coffee mug over Llewellyn's iffy wedding suit.

There was a moment's stunned silence, broken only by the drip, drip, drip of tepid black coffee.

Before Llewellyn could say a word, Rafferty soaked him for a second time – with a torrent of apologies rather than coffee. In some ways, it was the hardest part of the whole business; he only hoped his non-existent actor's skills proved convincing.

After the first flood of apology, Rafferty rushed to the kitchen to get a cloth. Returning with a tea towel, he began dabbing ineffectually at the most soggy areas of the jacket. 'God, I'm sorry,' he said again. 'What a clumsy git I am. I don't know how it happened. And you wanted to look so smart what with Superintendent Bradley going to the wedding and all.'

Llewellyn gave him a furious look and muttered, 'He's not coming. You know that perfectly well. I did tell you.'

Rafferty stopped his ineffectual dabbing and gaped at

him. 'Not coming? What do you mean, he's not coming? And for the record, you didn't tell me.' It was hardly something he'd be likely to forget.

Llewellyn snatched the tea towel and recommenced the dabbing. 'Yes, I did. I remember very well telling you he replied to the invitation immediately. Had the refusal delivered by hand. Maureen's mother was extremely put out.' His head was bent and he didn't notice Rafferty's expression as he added, 'But you've seemed a bit preoccupied lately. You probably weren't listening.'

Rafferty's reply was a strangled, 'No. I don't believe I was.'